I

SAID

YES

KIERSTEN MODGLIN

www.kierstenmodglinauthor.com

Cover Design: Tadpole Designs

Editing: Three Owls Editing

Proofreading: My Brother's Editor

Formatting: Tadpole Designs

First Print Edition: 2020

First Electronic Edition: 2020

To you, dear reader,
for saying yes to this book and supporting my dream.

CHAPTER ONE

HER

"Are you ready?" The officer stares me down with harsh eyes as he waits for me to stand. There is no real question in his words. Ready or not, it is my time to go. My time to face all that I've done.

I nod my head, standing from the uncomfortable bench in my tiny cell. "Yes."

I turn around as he approaches me so he can place the cuffs on my wrists, the sting of the metal on my bones so familiar I almost ache for them when they are gone. Like the wedding ring I once fiddled with every time I grew nervous. If it were still on my finger now, I am sure I would've managed to saw the digit clean off.

"Your lawyer is just down the hall." His tone is harsh, though his eyes seem kinder than the other officers' have been. He opens the door slowly, pushing me through it while holding tightly to the cuffs. We walk through the corridor in silence, each step taunting me as we grow closer to the place where I'll have to talk about what happened for the first time since that night.

Can I do it?

Better question, do I have any other choice?

When we reach the door to the room where my lawyer is waiting, the officer pulls on the cuffs. "Whoa," he says, slowing me down in the same manner you would a horse. "In here." He pushes open the door and walks me through.

The room is smaller than I expected, though I recognize the large mirror on the wall and the small table in the middle of the room from the numerous detective shows Mark and I used to watch.

Mark. Oh, how just the thought of his name pains me. Just the mere thought of his existence is enough to send me reeling back into the darkness that has consumed me for the past few weeks. I can't allow myself to go back there again.

My lawyer, a short, squat man who I've only met once before—and briefly at that—is seated at the table with an iPhone plastered to his ear, and he does not look happy.

His thin lips are pressed into a tight line, and he groans. "Fine, just…do what you can. Send those to me either way." With that, he pulls the phone from his ear, presses a button on its greasy screen, and stands up. The hair on his wrists sticks out from under the edge of his suit jacket as he crosses his arms over his plump belly. "Hannah." He greets me by a first name I've never given him permission to use, though he seems to know it's the one I prefer. "Nice to see you again."

I nod, though I don't bother returning the nicety. We both know it's far from nice to see each other—though I suppose it *is* nice for him, after all. I am sure my parents are paying him a pretty penny to be here for me.

2

He extends an arm, motioning for me to sit in the chair across from him. I do so dutifully, the metal of my cuffs sliding against the chair. I feel hands on my arms and hear the keys rattling as my wrists are freed. I throw my arms forward feverishly, rubbing my raw wrists and already missing the cuffs, despite the pain they've caused. The officer takes a few steps back before receiving an encouraging nod from my lawyer. "Thank you. That will be all for now. I believe we have a full hour."

Needing no further instruction, the officer walks from the room. Once the door has shut, my lawyer takes a deep breath, his large mustache wiggling.

He grins at me in a way that should be friendly but only seems creepy. "Now that he's gone, we can get more comfortable, can't we? How are you feeling?"

I chew on my bottom lip, placing my hands on the table and digging my fingernails into my palm. "Nervous," I admit.

"That's normal," he tells me, setting his phone down on the tabletop and opening the green folder in front of him. Sitting right on top is a giant picture of my mugshot. I grimace and force my eyes away from the picture and the memories that come with it. If I go there, I will break. I have to hold it together. "So, what I want to do today is just go over a few of the details. We need to work on preparing our case to go to trial, if that's what you want. I think we have a good shot at a better plea deal than they've offered, but I want to hear what you have to say before we make any decisions." He pauses, letting out a breath through his nose. "Okay?"

"Okay," I say, trying to still my shaking voice.

He pulls a pen from an inside pocket of his charcoal blazer and clicks it. "So, start from the beginning. Tell me what happened the night of the murder."

CHAPTER TWO

"Are you ready?" the officer asks, opening up the door to my cell. I'm not, but I nod anyway. I stand from the metal chair they have bolted to the floor and turn around, allowing him to place a pair of handcuffs on my wrists. The asshole tightens them on purpose, but I don't dare flinch to let him know it hurts. He wants to see my weakness, and I refuse to give him the satisfaction. "This way," he tells me, pulling me out of the cell and down the hall.

He stops us in front of a metal door and, without knocking, pushes it open. At a small metal table in the center of the room, sits a large, red-faced man. He is reading through a pad of scrawled-out notes in front of him, but when we enter, he stands and turns the paper over so I can't see what it says.

"Hello," he greets me. "It's nice to finally meet you, Mark."

I grumble a brief greeting before the officer sits me down at the table and removes my handcuffs. I'm no

5

longer seen as a threat in this room, apparently. The lawyer takes a seat after I do and clicks the pen in his hand. "My name's Brock Cavendish." He holds out his hand to shake mine, and I hesitate before extending him the same courtesy. I wait until his eyes show doubt and I can tell he's feeling foolish. He needs to know I'm the one with all the power here, even now.

When the officer has left the room, Brock Cavendish clears his throat. "Now then, I've just spoken with Hannah." *Hannah.* The name stings in the back of my throat like hour-old vomit, but I force it out of my mind as quickly as it enters. She has no place there anymore. No. I can't go there. Won't. I am surviving in this hellhole, thriving even, strictly thanks to my ability to shut things off—emotions, in particular. It's always been a strength of mine.

"Before we dive in, I wanted to say thank you for agreeing to meet with me. I needed to sit down with you today and discuss the case against both you and Hannah, see what I can learn from either of you. Now, you've probably been told, but your representation is covered— her parents have taken care of that. I expect you'll be hearing from your lawyer within days, but whatever you can tell me to help clear up some things would be very helpful."

I nod. "Okay." I need to clear my name. He needs to know how everything went wrong. He needs to know the truth about her and everything that happened, all of it.

"So," he flips the page to a blank one so quickly I can't even catch a glimpse of whatever he's trying to hide, "tell me about the night of the murder."

CHAPTER THREE

HER

THEN

I n the beginning, there was only light. I was on a work trip in Atlanta when my flight was delayed and I had to stay an extra night. Work trips were usually done by groups of us, but that trip I'd made alone.

I remember walking into the bar that would change my life as if it were just yesterday. It was dark and musty, and the outside noise of the street was immediately silenced as the heavy door shut behind me. I remember catching my reflection in the mirror behind the bar, my face illuminated by the neon signs that hung behind the barkeep.

I made my way across the red, carpeted stairs and onto the concrete floor, my heels clicking loudly and drawing unwanted attention my way. A waiter with a tray of drinks hurried past me without a second glance, though his felt like the only eyes that *weren't* on me. I took refuge at the bar, sinking onto a bar stool and laying my phone down on the wood. The bartender approached me, his thick eyebrows raised in surprise.

"Well, you aren't from around here, are you?"

"Is it that obvious?" I asked with a half-laugh.

He smirked. "I haven't seen anyone wearing a suit come through those doors since the day it opened. What can I get ya?"

"Scotch on the rocks with a twist, please," I said, staring at my phone as the notifications began to roll in. An email from my boss one minute, then two replies from others CC'd on said email. A text from a coworker. A text from a client. I turned the phone over. One minute. Just *one minute*—I just needed a minute to breathe.

"Long day?" he asked as he slid the drink across the counter and rested on his elbow in front of me.

"They're all long," I admitted, taking a sip and welcoming the warmth that flooded my chest. It *had* been a long day, if I were being honest. Longer than most. Starting with a flight that included a six-hour layover and ending with two client meetings with one of the toughest hospital CEOs I'd ever met, I was getting ready to board a plane and sleep for the next few hours when I was notified that I wouldn't be able to get home that night.

Home. It was a strange concept to me, I guess. The place I lived, the address where my mail was sent, was a tiny studio apartment in Seattle with very little to make it feel like an actual home. I slept in hotel beds more often than my own, and I had to think really hard to be able to tell you the color of my walls. I was in my home just a few short weeks a year, and it cost more than I'd like to admit to maintain it, but it was nice to have a place to go during the limited free time I was given. So, not being able to go home that night had been the very large bow on my already shitty day.

"So," he asked, interrupting my thoughts, "are you new to the area or in town for vacation?"

"Neither," I said in between sips. The drink was already almost gone. I took the last gulp and slid it back to him. "I'm in Atlanta for work. I head out in the morning."

"Hopefully not too early in the morning," he said, wiggling the empty glass in the air before he refilled it.

"I'll be okay," I said, taking the drink from him. It was true. Years of schmoozing alcoholic CEOs had trained me well. I knew my limits, and I knew how to avoid a hangover like the plague. With scotch, I could have four with plenty of water before even the slightest morning headache would affect me.

My phone buzzed again, and I let out a sigh before flipping it over. Another email. Four more meetings over the next two days. I guess I wasn't going home tomorrow after all. I scrolled through the email. New Orleans tomorrow, then Houston, and two in Tokyo on the second day. I pinched the bridge of my nose with stress.

"Not good news, I'm guessing," the bartender said, staring at my troubled expression with concern. I'd been so lost in my thoughts I'd forgotten he was there.

"It's fine," I said with a forced smile. "Just part of the job."

"What do you do?"

"I'm a pharmaceutical rep." His blank stare of confusion was entirely too familiar. "I sell medical devices and products to leading hospitals."

"Is it hard?" he asked.

"It's not…hard, I guess. It's, well, there are long hours and quite a bit of travel."

"But you get to see the world?" he asked.

"The hospitals of the world, at least," I joked. "There isn't much time for exploring the cities I visit. It's usually in one hospital and straight onto the next flight to the next city and the next hospital."

"If you hate it so much, why do it?" he challenged.

"I don't hate it," I argued.

"Well, you don't seem to like it all that much."

Fair enough. I squinted my eyes at him. Truth was, I didn't hate my job. Most days, I loved it. It was excellent money, I did get to travel, and the team I worked with made the trips we took together enjoyable. But, like most jobs, it came with its share of challenges. "Do you like *your* job?"

"I do," he said, picking up a glass from the rack behind him and wiping it dry before placing it on the shelf underneath the bar. "It's decent money, and I get to meet a ton of interesting people."

"Don't you get tired of dealing with drunk people?"

"Don't *you?*"

"Drunk people are more likely to buy my products," I said with a wink.

"Funny you should say that. Mine, too," he said. "Case in point." He stepped away from me quickly as a pair of men dressed in all leather approached the bar, their scraggly white beards shaking as they laughed loudly.

"'Nother round, Marky Mark. 'Nother round," the larger one shouted joyfully. I watched his spit fly into the air as he spoke, but the bartender didn't flinch. It was obvious he had a rapport with this particular customer.

"You got it, Tony," he said. The bartender, who I was just learning was named Mark, laid out four glasses and poured whiskey into them. The customer slid a hundred-dollar bill across the bar. "Keep the change." He laughed loudly—at God knows what—and the two took their drinks, walking away and back to their table as half their drinks sloshed out onto the floor.

When they'd moved out of earshot, Mark walked back to me. "See," he said, holding up the cash as he slid it into the register and began to pull out change for his tip.

"That was like," I tried to do the mental math, "at least a twenty-dollar tip." I was shocked, I had to admit. This was not the type of place I'd expect to see tips that size.

"More like sixty," he said, holding out three twenties and sliding them into his pocket. "Tony and his guys come in a few nights a week and get plastered on our cheapest whiskey. Four or five rounds like that a night and with tips that just get bigger as they go—the way I see it, Tony practically pays for my tuition."

"You're in school?" I asked, cocking my head to the side. He had a rough look to him with dark clothes and messy, chestnut hair that made me think college was the last place he would be. "What for?"

"I'm third year law," he said, breaking eye contact modestly.

"Seriously?"

He nodded, leaning forward on the bar in front of me. He was close enough I could smell his warmly scented cologne. "Yep, seriously. Why?"

"That's…impressive," I admitted, taking another drink of my scotch. I'd come into the conversation feeling superior, but as my cheeks lit on fire, I realized how quickly the tables had turned.

"It's no big deal," he said. "But thanks." He was quiet for a moment and then said, "Hey, I never got your name."

"It's Hannah," I told him, extending a hand. He leaned forward and accepted mine. It sounds cheesy, but when his skin touched mine, I swear I could feel the electricity pulsing between us. "Nice to meet you."

"*Very* nice to meet you," he agreed. "Look, I get off here in just a few minutes. I know you said you have an early flight and—" My phone's buzzing interrupted his words, and he glanced down. "I can see that you're busy, but…I'd love to hang out with you for a while. Would that be possible?"

"Oh, um—" I bit my lip nervously as my phone buzzed again. "I don't know. I, um—"

He nodded, tossing a towel over his shoulder and stepping even further back. "Okay, no worries. You don't have to come up with an excuse."

My phone buzzed again, but I placed it face down on the bar, focusing all of my attention on him. "It's not an excuse, it's just…well, I would love to go, but I don't come to Atlanta often. Ever, actually."

"But you're here tonight." His crystal blue eyes locked with mine in the dim bar light, and I sucked in a breath. No one had ever taken my breath away the way he did.

"But I may not ever be again. What happens after tonight?"

He chuckled under his breath. "I didn't just propose

marriage. I just wanted a burger and thought it might be nice to not be alone."

"Sorry to disappoint you, but I'm not a one-night stand kind of girl," I said firmly, setting the empty glass down and running a finger across the rim.

He furrowed his brow, placing a hand in front of his mouth. "Am I—am I not speaking clearly? I *thought* I said I wanted to take you to get something to eat, but apparently you heard drunken sexcapade and maybe even marriage proposal in there somewhere." He laughed, waving his hands in front of him casually. "Seriously, there's no pressure. If you don't want to go, just say so."

I twisted my mouth in thought. "I never said I don't want to go."

He grinned, patting the bar with his palm. "All right, then. It's settled. Give me fifteen minutes."

———

An hour later, Mark had cleaned up from his shift and we were in a small, quiet diner across town. The black-and-white tile floor reminded me of a restaurant from several decades before, but Mark assured me they had the best burgers in Atlanta, and who was I to argue?

By the time the waiter brought us our food, my stomach was growling for sustenance. It had been years since I'd allowed myself anything as tempting as a greasy fry, but as I picked it up, I began to wonder why.

I let out an embarrassing moan as soon as the fry touched my tongue, and Mark snorted. I felt my cheeks turning pink, from the warmth of the food, his attention, and the self-consciousness I felt for eating like a pig in front of him.

"I told you it was good," he said.

"It's not that. I mean, it *is* good, it's just...I don't really eat *this stuff*. I forgot how good it was."

"This stuff?" he asked, one brow raised as he glanced to his plate. "Food?"

"Food that's bad for me. I'm kind of a food addict." To my surprise, he didn't take one look at my thin figure and argue with me like most people did when they learned my secret. "I used to be much bigger. It took me a long time to lose the weight, and I haven't let myself go back to the old way of eating for fear of losing control and gaining it all back."

His expression turned instantly serious. "I'm so sorry, Hannah," he said, pushing his plate away from him. "I should've asked. Do you want to go somewhere else?"

"No," I assured him. "Honestly, it's fine. This is...good for me. A healthy relationship with food and all, right?"

He didn't look so sure. "You aren't going to offend me if you don't want to eat this. I don't want to be the thing that causes you to falter with your progress. They probably have salads here...what do you eat?"

"Salads, mostly," I said, squeezing the fry between my fingers until its insides exploded before placing it down on my plate.

"Why didn't you say anything?" he asked. His tone wasn't accusatory as much as curious.

"You were so excited about *Atlanta's best burger and fries*, I didn't want to disappoint you."

He looked down and sucked in a breath, then stood

from the booth, grabbed our plates, and walked toward the counter. When he returned a few minutes later, he had two salads in his hand. "Here, Atlanta's best salad."

"You didn't have to do that," I said, worried he was angry.

"I'm an alcoholic, Hannah," he said matter-of-factly. "An alcoholic who works in a bar. If anyone understands temptation, it's me. So, you're going to have to be gentle with my addiction," he paused, "and I'll be gentle with yours."

With that, he dug into his salad without another word. It was the simplest gesture, and yet bigger than a dozen roses. In that small moment, I'm pretty sure the first piece of my heart began to fall for him.

CHAPTER FOUR

HER

Our relationship moved quickly. After that first date, we kept in contact despite my demanding work schedule and his equally demanding school schedule. Phone calls were exchanged, and any chance I had to make a pit stop in Atlanta, I took it.

After six months of this exhausting exchange, Mark asked me to move in with him. The thought was terrifying. I had a good job, though it was admittedly getting more frustrating to be away from him for weeks at a time, and I'd never been a fan of warm weather or the stereotypes that came with living in the South, but I loved Mark. Despite everything I was unsure of, I was so sure of that. I could do my job based out of anywhere, but he was nearly finished with school and wasn't in a place where he could transfer. We could've waited a few months and reevaluated after he'd graduated, but we were crazy kids in love, and nothing could keep us apart any longer. Without allowing myself to think of all the reasons it could've been a bad idea, I said yes, agreed to take that step, and the decision was made.

A month after that, everything I owned was being unloaded by movers into Mark's cozy two bedroom townhome. Things in the South were more affordable, at least.

I remember Mark asking me if I was happy I'd moved home with him. *Home.* It was already my home before I'd unpacked the first box. Though I'd been unsure about it up until that point, hearing those words from him was all that I needed to seal the deal. I was home. *He* was my home. For a girl who lived on the road, having a home was a really good feeling.

In the beginning, things were great. I flew home to Atlanta a few times a month, a few times a week if we were really lucky, and despite the strain, we made the best of the moments we had together. Mark would always request off the nights we knew I'd be home and we'd go out together, exploring the city I was beginning to fall in love with.

I think the distance made things better between us, sometimes. There was never any time for the usual stupid fighting couples eventually do. We only had a limited amount of time together, and so we had to make the most of it. In theory, it should've been a mess, but somehow it just worked.

Another six months went by with that arrangement, and then, on the day Mark graduated, he asked me to marry him. The proposal happened in the middle of the lawn of his law school, surrounded by hooping and hollering classmates as they threw their caps in the air, celebrating their achievement. Despite the noise, it felt intimate, like we were the only people in the world. That's how it always felt with Mark, like the two of us were completely alone in the world. Nothing, no one, mattered but us. Looking back, I guess that's how he wanted it.

Despite feeling, in the moment, that we were the only people there, we were literally surrounded by screaming people. I was so sure I'd heard him wrong the first time that I had to ask him to repeat himself. He did, without hesitation. And I'd heard right.

I thought maybe he was just asking in the heat of the moment, but he pulled a ring from his pocket and proved me wrong again. As he kneeled to the ground, my eyes filled with tears and I began to cry. I couldn't even answer through the tears, but he seemed to understand.

"I love you," he whispered as he pulled me into his arms and kissed my lips.

"I love you, too," I choked out. No words had ever been more true.

Things were perfect. I'd never been happier than I was from the time we met until we got married. In the beginning, there was only light.

After the wedding, everything changed.

CHAPTER FIVE

HER

PRESENT DAY

The lawyer interrupts my words by clearing his throat. I blink from my trance, ghosts of memories in my eyes: the way it felt the first time Mark kissed me, the night we made love for the first time, the way he smelled when he'd come back from a run, the way he'd hold me close when we'd watch a movie together. Many, many moments—big and little, but good nonetheless. There is so much good in our love story. *So much.* I want him to see that, but I know he won't. No one will see it now, once they hear our story, but it was there. Despite it all, it is *still* there. He lays his pen down for a moment and smiles at me sadly.

"You know you don't have to tell me everything, Hannah. Not if it doesn't affect the case."

I nod. I do know. I could tell him what he wants to hear—about *that* night—and be done with it, but it isn't that simple. Nothing's ever really that simple, is it? Yes, I remember it all. Yes, it's all my fault. Yes. Yes. Yes.

But it's not a simple yes or no. Not this time. There's always a why. Within *my* why is the story of our love and where it all went wrong. And it's a story worth telling, so if he wants to hear the truth, he'll have to sit through the whole thing.

"I know," I say finally, clasping my hands on the table in front of me. "But I think you have to hear it all. You won't understand if not."

He nods, picking his pen back up and allowing me to continue. "So, you met your husband two years ago?"

"Mhm," I say. "Three in May."

"And you two were married just a year later?"

"A year and three months."

"And you say the marriage went sour pretty quickly?"

Sour. As if we were a bad batch of grapes. As if the two of us, our lives intertwined, could be reduced to a poor produce choice that you would throw out with the garbage. I nod stiffly, not bothering to argue. Does it matter anymore? "Yes."

"Okay, go on. Tell me more about how things changed so quickly."

CHAPTER SIX

HIM

PRESENT DAY

The lawyer turns over the paper in his notebook, ready for the next page. He stares at me, his mouth pressed into such a thin line it almost disappears.

"Tell me about Hannah," he says.

I grit my teeth, my blood boiling with anger. "What about her?"

"Tell me how you met."

"You know how we met," I say. He thinks he can play me, that I'm a fool, but he's wrong. He'll know that soon enough.

"I'd like for you to tell me anyway," he presses on, and I can feel the vein in my temple pulsing.

My heart thuds in my chest, an angry warning that he is asking too many questions. What does he know? What has she told him about me? What filthy lies has she spewed from that putrid mouth? "You shouldn't trust her," I say finally. If I say much more, I'll explode.

The lawyer looks at me with a strange expression, one hairy eyebrow higher than the other. "What makes you say that?"

"She's a liar. That's all she is. She'll manipulate you into doing whatever she wants—believing whatever she wants you to believe. And she'll destroy your life in the process. You think you know her, but you don't. You don't know what she's capable of."

"Damon—"

"*Mark*," I correct furiously. "I don't go by my first name."

He clears his throat. "Right. *Mark.* Sorry. Can you tell me something specific about why you believe Hannah is a liar?"

I listen to his tone and the way he stares at me, and I already know the truth. I see the way he fiddles with his watch while I talk, as if he'd rather be anywhere else. He doesn't believe me. Not a word I'm saying. I can see it all over his face. That's when I realize she's already gotten to him. He interviewed her first, listened to all of her lies, and now, I stand no chance. Women are so pure and innocent, aren't they? It's always the men who lie, right? Wrong. Hannah's the best liar there is. I never stood a chance as long as she was involved.

"Mark—"

I pound my fists on the table angrily to shut him up. "*What does it matter?*" I scream. "What's the point? You don't believe me. I can see it all over your face. You don't give a *fuck* what I say about any of it. You've already got your story, don't you? The innocent little housewife already spun you her web of lies, and you took to it like a fly." Too late for him. Too late for me. I can feel the anger rising to the surface. The first explosion was just a splash in the bath compared to the tsunami that is coming if he doesn't watch himself. No one ever listens to me. No one wants to see the truth, not where she's involved. She seems more trustworthy, I get it, but I know better. I know her so well.

"Now that's not true," he says. "I want to hear your version, Mark. I want to hear what happened."

CHAPTER SEVEN

HER

THEN

"How was work?" I asked as Mark hurried in the door with a bright smile plastered on his face. He seemed happy, the happiest I'd seen him in a while.

"Fantastic," he said, laughter filling his voice. "This place is...amazing, Han. The partners are going to be great to work for, I can already tell. I have a real office there—I can't wait for you to see it—and I have my own secretary, *a door*, a separate phone line. It feels like it's all coming together." He held his arms out and scooped me up as I walked toward him, spinning me around and kissing my lips. He planted his hand firmly on my butt as our kiss grew more intense. All too soon, he pulled away. "All we've worked for, babe, it's finally happening."

"I'm so happy you had a good day," I told him, rubbing my thumb over my lips. It was true. Mark had been working for a small, not-for-profit law firm as his first job straight out of college, and though he'd never been one to seem greedy, I knew it was taxing work. He'd been working long hours with little pay and too many clients to keep track of for months. When a position opened up at Lyman and Associates, we knew it was a long shot. When he actually *got* the position, we were both shocked. I'd been half expecting him to come home and tell me it was all a prank.

"Good doesn't even cover it. The best, that's more like it. The best day imaginable. I've got so much to tell you. We need wine," he said, setting me down on my feet and hurrying past me. "Something to celebrate."

"Wine?" I asked, shocked by his words. It took me a half-second to process because it was so out of character. It was then that I recognized the strange taste on his lips. *Champagne.* "Have you been drinking?"

"I had a glass," he said with a shrug. "No big deal. They opened a bottle at work, and I didn't want to be rude."

I furrowed my brow at him, following as he dismissed me on his way to the kitchen. "Mark, you're an alcoholic. You shouldn't be drinking."

He pulled open the door to the refrigerator but shut it and turned around to face me without getting anything out. "Thank you very much for telling me about my own ailment, Han. I hadn't realized." There was a smirk still on his face, but it was fading fast.

"It's true. You shouldn't be drinking. You've done so well—"

"Yes, *I* have. And if *I* choose to have a glass of champagne to celebrate years of hard work, why shouldn't I?"

"You know as well as I do, one glass leads to one hundred. You've said it a million times. It's why you worked at a bar. So you could build up a tolerance for being around it and not be tempted. So you could handle being offered alcohol without having to say yes."

"I *can* handle it," he said indignantly. "This time was different, okay? I'm new. I couldn't say no, Hannah. It would've been rude, or embarrassing at least. It's fine. I'm fine. It was just one glass."

"You just asked for one more!" I yelled, slamming my hands to my sides.

He sucked in a breath. "Well, fucking excuse me for thinking you'd want to celebrate with me on the biggest day of my career." He shoved past me, hurrying from the kitchen in a cloud of anger.

"Since when do we celebrate with alcohol?" I asked. I myself had given up drinking around the house to help ease his temptation.

"Well, we can't celebrate with anything else good, can we?" he screamed back from the other room.

I hurried after him, following him up the stairs and to our bedroom. "What the hell does that mean?"

He was fuming by the time I reached him, his hands shaking as he unbuttoned his dress shirt. "Just that every once in a while I'd like to have a slice of pizza or, *god forbid*, a piece of cake."

"I never said you couldn't—"

"It's the unspoken rule, isn't it? None of us gets what we want around here."

I stepped back as if he'd slapped me as hard as his words stung. "What's *that* supposed to mean?"

His head hung down as he pulled the shirt from his back, wadding it into a ball and tossing it into the hamper

26

across the room. He shook his head. "Nothing, forget it. I didn't mean that."

"What exactly did you mean, then?" I asked.

He stepped toward me, the anger suddenly gone. "I didn't mean anything, Han. Sorry. I just...I was in a good mood, and you're right, I shouldn't have had anything to drink. I don't like the version of me that I am when I drink. You deserve better."

"I don't want to limit what you eat. I'm a grown woman, Mark. I can resist temptation. If you want pizza or cake, by all means—"

"I don't," he said quickly, cutting me off. "My waistline thanks you for the changes you've made to my diet." He patted his stomach, then kissed the top of my head. "I'm sorry, I don't want to fight with you. I have so much to tell —" He stopped, his eyes locking on something across the room, and I felt my reclaimed happiness dissipating as I realized what it was.

"Are you leaving?" he asked, staring at the suitcase in the corner.

"I have to catch a flight at nine."

His face fell. "To where?"

"Denver. It's just two days. I'll be home for the weekend."

"I thought you'd gotten the whole week off?" he asked.

"I thought so too, but this meeting came up last minute and there were no other reps to take it. It's a sale we really need." When I could see he wasn't cheering up, I went on. "Besides, you're going to be at work all week, anyway. It's not like me sitting at home is doing anyone any good."

"As opposed to you being on an airplane?"

"As opposed to me making money," I argued, poking his chest playfully. When he didn't smile, I groaned. "Why are you making a big deal about this?"

"Well, first of all, because you didn't tell me."

"I just found out a few hours ago. I was going to tell you when you got home."

"And, second of all, because I thought you'd be home to hear about my new job. This is such a big step for me. It's all we've worked for…" He trailed off, his eyes dancing between mine as he begged me to understand. I did understand. I knew what the day meant to him, but I had a job to do, too.

"And I am here, Mark. I'm right here. I don't have to leave for a few hours. You can tell me all about your day, we'll have dinner, and then when I get home, we can go out for the weekend and really celebrate."

He nodded, but I could see his spirits were only partially lifted. "Whatever." He pulled the undershirt over his head and grabbed the loose T-shirt he slept in from the end of the bed.

"Don't be angry," I said. "I want to hear more about your new job."

He pulled on his pajama pants and took my hand, pulling me to his lap as he sat on the edge of the bed. His kiss was slower and he seemed to have finally given up the last of his anger. "I'll tell you in a minute. First, let me give you something to remember me by."

CHAPTER EIGHT

HER

I worked for another few months at my job before it became such an issue that I agreed to quit. By that time, Mark was making enough money for us to live on, and my traveling seemed to be causing the greatest rift in our marriage. It felt like the right thing to do. I won't say I wasn't bitter about it—I loved my job despite its many flaws—but I loved Mark more, and when I had to make the choice, there was no true competition.

One day a few months after I'd begun staying at home full time, I was preparing a load of laundry. I grabbed handfuls of dirty clothes from the hamper in our bedroom and transferred them into the larger hamper from our laundry room. As I did, something purple fell from the pile of clothes, catching my eye.

I stopped almost instantly, staring down to where the shiny object had fallen, knowing what it was without having to inspect it. I moved a pair of slacks that were blocking my view and, sure enough, there it was. The condom lay on the floor—it wasn't completely unusual, it was the brand we used, but why had it been in with his dirty laundry? They had no reason to leave our bedroom.

My first reaction wasn't to accuse him of an affair. The first emotion I remember feeling was that of true confusion. How had it gotten there? I dug through the basket to no avail. There were no more waiting to be found. Next, I checked his underwear drawer where we always kept a box. It was there, right where it always was.

I pulled the box out, counting the number of condoms we had left—six. When was the last time we'd replaced them? I couldn't remember. Suddenly, my mind was filled with anger as the realization that this could point to an affair hit me. Was it possible? Could I picture Mark cheating? He'd been distant since starting his job, but our sex life was great. Aside from the usual things couples fought about, we had a good marriage. What reason could he have for straying?

I pulled my phone from the pocket of my oversized sherpa cardigan and clicked on the green icon that would take me to my recent calls. His name was at the top of the list. I clicked on it, watching the screen turn dark as the line began to ring.

I waited, chewing my lip and pacing the bedroom floor, my feet rubbing lines in the carpet.

He answered on the third ring, and I felt an unfamiliar sting of tears fill my eyes at the sound of his voice. How could he betray me? How could he do it? "Hello?"

"M-mark?" I asked.

"Hannah?" He sounded distant. Distracted.

I realized in that moment I had no plan of attack. I had no idea what I was going to say to him, though I was ready to give him a piece of my mind. I needed to be calm. Rational. I didn't need to accuse him of anything until I had more proof. Thoughts plagued my mind—all the things I could say, all the things I shouldn't. I knew Mark. I knew if I went in headfirst with accusations and questions, his wall would go up and I'd get nothing out of him. Instead, I had to play it smart, despite all the pain and emotion begging me not to. I wanted answers, but there was only one way to get them with him and this wasn't it.

"What is it?" he asked, obvious concern in his voice for the first time.

"S-sorry. I just, um, I wondered what time you were planning to be home? I was thinking of running into town to see my mom, but I want to be home when you get here."

He mumbled something under his breath, and I heard his hand swish over the microphone as he said something indiscernible to someone in the background. "Yeah, that's fine," he said finally. "Go out with your friend or whatever. I'll be at work late, anyway."

I rolled my eyes at the fact that he hadn't even heard my request. "Okay, thanks."

"Was that it? Sorry, honey, I'm right in the middle of something." His tone now lacked the concern he'd been showing before. He was back to work before I'd given him the okay.

"Yeah, that was it. Sorry to bother you," I muttered.

"Talk to you soon, Han. Gotta go." With that, the line went dead, and I was left alone, still holding the purple condom wrapper.

I tossed the packet back in the drawer with disgust,

not sure whether to be angry or proud of myself for not asking him about it. Finally, I strode past the hamper on my way out the door of the bedroom. I pulled up the banking app on my phone, scrolling through our latest transactions. It was something I rarely did—Mark handled the finances. I know it sounds old school, but it worked. I still had access to everything. My name was on every account, but he made sure the money was always there and I never had to question it. At least, I'd had no reason to question until now. Now, I had every reason to second guess our unspoken arrangement.

I scrolled through the transactions, looking for anything unusual. Trips to the gas stations, lunches at local restaurants, bills being paid. Nothing screamed strange to me, not right out of the gate. I let out a breath. Okay. That was a good sign.

The next step was to check his computer. I walked into the office across the hall from our bedroom. Truly, it was an extra bedroom, but with just the two of us, he'd managed to turn it into an office, and I hadn't complained. Someday, I hoped it would be a nursery, and God knows what he would do with his monstrosity of a desk, but that was an argument for a different day.

I opened the silver MacBook Air, typing in the password he used for all of his devices. The lock screen disappeared, allowing me access to a version of him I very rarely saw. The computer held the websites he visited when I was fast asleep, the apps he'd downloaded to entertain him when I couldn't, and the music and podcasts he listened to with headphones on to shut me out. I'd always held a slight resentment toward his computer—he spent far too much time furiously typing away on it with the rest of the world, *me*, shut out.

That day, none of it mattered. I was thankful that I had a version of him tucked away for me to rifle through when things were bad. I had no idea how bad things were going to get.

First, I checked his browsing history: Facebook, of course, a few legal forums, YouTube, and GoogleDocs. There was nothing suspicious—I'd have to dig deeper. I opened up his Facebook and checked his messages. Nothing out of the ordinary. Next, I pulled up Google-Docs—what trouble could he really get into on YouTube? —and searched through legal documents he'd worked up. I shouldn't have snooped. It was none of my business, and he'd made that clear. His clients had a right to privacy, even from me. But at that moment, I didn't care. I wanted to know the truth about my husband and about our marriage. Was it in jeopardy? If so, why?

As I scrolled through the documents, one in particular caught my eye. It was labeled Untitled and the thumbnail showed it was shorter than the rest of the documents. I clicked to open it up and read through the brief letter. It wasn't addressed to anyone, yet it was very obviously written to a specific person.

I don't know what you want from me, but what I can offer is money. A lot of it. If you will both agree to sign a non-disclosure, in perpetuity, then I will pay you whatever you'd like. Send your terms to moliver@Ly-manandAssociates.com by end of day Friday and we can discuss this.

That was it. I read over it twice. Who could the letter

be to, and what was it about? What great secret could he be withholding that he'd offer up our personal finances to keep it under wraps? It made no sense.

Before I could stop myself, I clicked the printer icon in the top right corner and listened as the machine across the room fired up. I closed out of his computer and grabbed the paper as I hurried out of the room. I didn't know what I'd uncovered—I had no idea what I was about to find, but I did know I'd found something and I wasn't about to be the stupid, doting housewife who thinks her husband could do no wrong.

If that was who he thought he'd married, he'd know soon enough how wrong he was.

CHAPTER NINE

HER

I hid the letter in the bottom of my dresser drawer as I tried to come up with a plan. That night, when Mark arrived home from work, I put on a fake smile as I placed a plate in front of him. It was all I could do to bite my tongue, but it felt like the best plan at the time.

Would things have been different if I'd confronted him right then?

Would things have ended differently?

If I'd done so, would I still be sitting in prison telling this story?

I guess I'll never know.

Before we'd begun eating, he stood up and walked to the fridge. He pulled out a bottle of wine, one I hadn't noticed he'd stored in the back. "Did you have fun with your friend?" he asked, noticing me eyeing the bottle.

"My mom," I corrected.

"Hmm?" He pulled a glass down from the cabinet and filled it quickly. "Do you want some?"

"It was my mom that I was meeting. Anyway, I didn't end up going. And…no. No, thank you."

He shrugged, shoving the cork back into the bottle, though we both knew he'd be back to finish it off before the meal ended. "Suit yourself." It did no good to argue with him, try as I might. The sober man I'd married what seemed like just a few months before that was gone. The man that sat across from me now was practically a stranger.

"How was your day?" I asked as he took the first sip. I wondered how much he'd already had to drink throughout the day. It wasn't long ago that I took a swig of his water bottle only to discover it was vodka he was taking to work with him. It was rare that he came home to me without the taste of alcohol on his lips, though he showed no signs of being drunk until he'd had a few glasses of his drink of choice at home.

"Fine," he said, stabbing his fork into the plate of alfredo. "This looks great, babe." He took a bite and nodded—to confirm, I supposed. "Actually, it was a shit day, if I'm being honest. My clients are," he grimaced, his eyes going dark as he drifted off to think of them, "hor- rible people."

"Do you have to represent them?" I asked mindlessly, twirling my fork in the noodles. Truth be told, my mind was on the letter still, and I had no extra capacity to take in what he was saying.

"'Course I do. Lyman doesn't care about their charac- ter, he cares about their pockets. And their pockets run deep." The wine glass was empty already, though I hadn't been able to watch him drink most of it. "Something wrong?" he asked, one brow raised. It was almost a test. He thought the drinking was what was upsetting me, and he was waiting to see if I was going to say anything. As much as I wanted to, I knew it would do no good. Financially, working at Lyman and Associates was the best thing that could've happened to us. In every other aspect of our lives, it ruined us. He'd taken his first drink in years on his first day and never looked back. Still, I couldn't let him believe any different. Not if my plan was going to work. He had to think I was *only* upset about his drinking.

"Sorry, no. I just…I'm not feeling very well. I think I'm going to go to bed." I pushed the untouched plate of food away from me.

"You've hardly eaten any of your food. Even your salad. You aren't getting a bug, are you?"

"I hope not," I said, holding my stomach instinctively. "I love you."

"Love you, too," he said, taking hold of my arm as I moved to pass him. "You sure you're okay?"

"Mhm," I said with a quick nod, hardly able to meet his eyes.

"Is this about the wine?" he pressed.

"No, honestly. I just…I'm not feeling well."

"You know I'm not going to let it control me," he assured me. It was a false promise if I'd ever heard one, but I couldn't argue. "It's different than before."

Again, I nodded, pulling my arm from his grasp. "I know. It's not that, honest."

"Okay," he said finally. "Just one glass tonight, I promise." He stood, kissing my forehead. "Can't afford to catch it," he explained. "Are you okay if I stay down here and work for a bit?"

"Yes," I said, secretly relieved. I wasn't sure how long I could keep quiet around him as my body remained on edge and ready to attack. Every time I'd stabbed my fork into my kale, I'd done so with a little extra force just to relieve the tension within myself. "I'll see you in the morning."

He squeezed my hand and, for just a second, I saw the man I'd fallen in love with. There was a kindness in his eyes that took me back to the early days of our relationship where there was only happiness and the cracks hadn't begun to show. Now, there seemed to be only cracks.

CHAPTER TEN

HER

I felt his lips brush my head, heard him telling me that he was leaving and that he'd see me later, but my eyes would barely open. It was as if saying I was sick had caused my immune system to get on board.

When I heard the bedroom door open and shut again, I opened my eyes. The clock on the nightstand showed that it was just past six. I sat up in bed and shook the covers off my legs, looking around. I searched my brain for memories from the day before—had it all been real? Was I really going to go through with the plan?

The sound of his car's engine starting up rang through the cracked window to my left, and I went into action. I pulled the ponytail holder from my wrist and tied my hair up into a quick, messy bun, glancing in the mirror just briefly enough to wipe the dark makeup from under my eyes. Next, I threw on a pair of jeans from the hamper I'd discarded the day before and a clean t-shirt from my drawer. I swiped on fresh deodorant and pushed a piece of mint gum in my mouth. It would have to do—I didn't have much time.

I pulled on sneakers as I rushed down the stairs and grabbed my purse and keys before I rushed out the door and into the garage. It was only a one-car, so we parked mine inside and kept his on the outside. He claimed it was because he wanted to be chivalrous, but I always suspected he didn't like the idea of my trusty Hyundai being parked on the curb where the neighbors couldn't get a good look at his Lexus. I climbed into the front seat and pushed the button to open the garage door, the sunshine reflecting in my rearview mirror and causing me to squint until I could locate my sunglasses.

I never thought I'd be the type of wife to trail my husband around, keeping track of his whereabouts. I'm not jealous, and I'm by no means a worrier, but something in the pit of my stomach was screaming something wasn't right. I had to trust that.

I turned out of our subdivision a few minutes later and hit the highway. I knew his route to work, so he should've only been a bit ahead of me. I weaved in between cars, trying to get an eye on him. For a moment, I worried I'd missed him, or that he'd chosen a different route. If that was the case, all of my planning would've been for nothing.

Luckily, as I reached a stoplight, I caught a glimpse of him about six cars ahead in the lane to my right. I felt my shoulders relax slightly. So far, so good. Now to just make sure I wasn't caught.

I kept my distance behind Mark as we drove through midtown traffic and headed for his office building. Luckily, his office downtown meant there'd be plenty of parking options and plenty of places to stay hidden. He pulled into the parking garage that we paid a small fortune per month for him to use, and his car disappeared. I turned left at the next street and pulled into a nearly full parking lot, advertising a rate of just seven dollars for the full day—thank God it was a weekday or the price would be triple that. I pulled cash from my pocket and fed it into the machine, fighting with a few stubborn bills. When the gate's arm lifted to allow me passage, I sped through and pulled into the last remaining spot on the edge of the lot, giving me an only partially obstructed view of the office building.

My stomach grumbled as I shut the car off, protesting the fact that I'd had to skip breakfast and hadn't run through anywhere to eat. I didn't have much cash and I couldn't risk Mark seeing a charge if I were to use my debit card. If I'd been smart, I would've packed a lunch, but it hadn't come to mind until right then. I rummaged around in the center console, pulling out another piece of gum and trading it out for more flavor.

I should've at least packed a water, but I wasn't thinking clearly. I flipped up the visor that had been blocking the sun and scooted forward in my seat, watching for Mark to exit the parking garage. It took longer than expected and, for a moment, I worried I missed him, but then, there he was. He walked across the busy street with just one glance in each direction.

There was a knot in my stomach that I couldn't deny. Every inch of my skin crawled with anticipation and dread. What would my day uncover? What did I want it to? I watched as he entered the high-rise building and pictured him climbing into the elevator and riding it up to the third floor, where he would spend his day.

Every pretty woman who walked into the building after him was a suspect. I stared them down, looking for a sign that they were the one who could ruin everything for me. The one who could make my husband risk everything.

I watched as the day ticked by, bouncing in my seat from a full bladder, but I didn't dare leave my post. I couldn't miss him. I couldn't miss the chance to catch whatever it was that would give me my answers. I put my sunglasses on as the midday sun broke through the clouds, causing a glare on the hood of my car. I half-considered giving up, but I was no quitter.

One time at work, they'd made us take a personality quiz. I can't remember the name of it. When the results came in, it showed my biggest personality trait, was that of a maximizer —someone who is all black or white, all in or all out. No room for gray. I'd never read anything more true, though I hadn't had a name for it before then. My maximizer person-ality would never let me do anything halfway. I was all in and I would sooner urinate on the floor than admit defeat.

Luckily, I didn't have to do either. At half past eleven, my husband strode out the front door of his office building with a blonde woman next to him. From what I could tell, she wasn't one of the women I'd seen entering the building that morning. Anger welled in my belly, enough to make me nauseous, and I felt fresh tears sting my eyes.

How could he do that to me? We weren't three years into our marriage, and already he'd betrayed me. Already he'd cast me aside like yesterday's news. How many times had there been? How many women? In that moment, I understood what people meant by the phrase 'blinded by rage.' My vision was blurring, both from tears and white-hot anger. I put the keys into the ignition, no longer aware of my plan, and revved the engine. I pulled from the parking spot as soon as I saw his car turning out of the parking garage.

I didn't care anymore if he saw me following him. He'd been caught red handed, and there was no way he could've talked himself out of this. I zipped around a car, gunning it through a yellow light to arrive behind him. His brake lights came on—had he seen me? He made a sudden left at the next street and I did the same, narrowly missing a car as it blared its horn at me. I didn't care. I cared about nothing at that moment. Nothing other than confronting my husband.

The black car came to a sudden stop in front of me, turning into a parking space on the street. My stomach fell, and I swallowed, pulling in just behind him. The driver's door to his car opened, and he shoved his leg out, his black dress shoes shining in the sun. He stepped out of the car, looking directly at me with a look of outright indignance.

"Hannah?" he called. "What the hell are you doing?" His voice was demanding as he threw his arms out to his sides.

"I should ask you the same thing," I spat, stepping out

of my car and marching toward him. He looked me up and down, obviously not impressed.

"You don't look well. Are you still feeling ill? Have you been to the doctor?" His face turned from anger to confusion. "Were you planning to surprise me for lunch?"

"Even if I was, it seems like you're a bit busy," I said, pursing my lips as if to show he'd been caught.

"What are you talking about?"

Unable to control myself any longer, my voice broke as I asked the question that was causing my insides to squirm. "Who is she, Mark?"

His jaw clenched, his mouth shoved to one side, as he stared at me. "Who is *who*? What are you talking about?" He glanced toward his car, following me as I pointed and marched toward where I knew she was waiting.

"The woman you're having an affair with. Don't play dumb with me." I stormed around toward the front of the car to glance through his window and gasped. To my surprise, there was no one in the car with him. I looked around me, convinced she was there. "Where did she go?"

"*She* who? What are you talking about, Han? Are you running a fever?" He approached me with caution, lifting an extended hand toward my forehead to check. I swatted it away.

"I'm fine. Where is the woman you were with?"

"*What woman?*" he demanded.

"The blonde that you left your office with. I know she was with you." Suddenly, it was hitting me how ridiculous I must look. What must he think of me, behaving this way?

"Leilani?" he asked, his jaw dropping down. "What,

were you…were you watching my office?" He rubbed a curled hand across his temple. "Were you *stalking* me? What is going on, Han?"

Fat tears filled my eyes as the adrenaline began to leave my body. "I found a condom in the laundry. I thought…I thought—" I couldn't finish the sentence.

"You thought I was having an affair?" he confirmed, his lips tight. Suddenly, he let out a laugh. "Hannah." He stepped forward, clicking his tongue and pulling me into his chest despite my protests. His breaths turned into laughter, and I looked up at him.

"What's so funny?"

He smirked. "You are…*plenty* of woman for me. What on earth would I need to go and have an affair for?"

"Then why were you with that woman?"

"Leilani is one of the junior partners. She's under Bill and Lonnie, but still my boss," he said. "We walked out of the building together because I was just finishing up with a meeting and she was leaving. She's married and twice my age. If I was going to have an affair, she certainly wouldn't be my prime choice. Besides, I'd never risk my job or our marriage like that. You know me. " He kissed my forehead, squeezing me tight. "Are you sure you're feeling all right?"

I nodded, though suddenly that wasn't true. The mounting pressure of the day was rolling over me as I realized how ridiculous I'd been. I wasn't *James Bond*. I was Hannah Oliver, and this little mission had done nothing but cause my bladder irreparable damage and my husband to think I was a lunatic.

"I'm sorry," I said. "I don't know what's come over me."

"You still feel warm," he said. I knew he was lying, though I wasn't sure if it was for my benefit or his. Sick as I felt, I wasn't feverish. Still, I let him lead me to my car. "Let's get you home."

"I need to take the car."

He waved me off. "I'll have it towed. You shouldn't be driving in your condition."

I nodded, sinking into his chest as we made it to the car and he opened the door. "Here you go," he said, placing me in the seat and buckling me in. He kissed my forehead again. "I love you, my crazy girl."

He shut the door, its impact reverberating across the car as my stomach let out another loud growl. How could I have been so foolish?

CHAPTER ELEVEN

HER

"I want to have a baby." We were sitting in our garden tub, bubbles up to our shoulders, the first time I mentioned it. I'd been toying with the idea for months, but it was only in the last several weeks that I'd worked up the courage to bring it up.

Despite all the plans we'd made before the wedding, plans for a future home and future careers, children had never come up. I'd never wanted to seem like I was moving too quickly, choosing to let Mark take the lead in all of our biggest decisions—moving in, getting married. But now, I wanted to make a decision for us. Kids were the next step.

He tossed a bit of bubbles at me playfully, his foot teasing my side. "Yeah, okay."

"I'm serious," I told him, scooting further up in the tub. "I'm here all day by myself. I get lonely. Now that I'm not working, wouldn't this be the perfect time to start trying?"

"If you're lonely, why don't we get a dog?"

I couldn't tell if he was joking or not, but his face showed no sign of a smile. "I don't want a dog. I'm not a dog person, you know that."

"Yes, I do, but I didn't know you were a kid person, either." He tossed more suds my way. "What if our kid wanted a dog?"

"We need a kid to have to worry about that, don't we?" I paused. "Are you...serious? You didn't think I'd want children?"

He shrugged.

"Don't *you* want us to have kids? A little boy you could teach how to play catch?"

"I've never really thought about it, I guess."

"How could you not think about it? It's our future." How could anyone not think about having children? I'd spent so many years dreaming of their little faces, the way they'd laugh, even the messes they'd make. I wanted it all, and lately the idea had been resurfacing more and more. I suppose my biological clock was letting me know it was time.

"I don't know, I guess I just never wanted kids. You've never mentioned them, so I thought you felt the same." He was no longer meeting my eyes as he spoke.

I glanced up at the ceiling as I tried to piece my thoughts together. What was happening? It was not at all how I'd expected the conversation to go. He was supposed to be excited, flip me over, and insist we start trying right then. How could he say he never wanted kids? Wasn't that the kind of thing you brought up before you marry someone? Doesn't everyone just assume both people want kids unless someone says otherwise? I couldn't believe it. "I...

well, I just thought it was a given, I guess. You don't want kids *at all*?"

"I just…I don't know. Kids complicate things, don't they?"

"Complicate things how?" I was drawing circles in the bubbles, watching my finger twirl round and round as it traced. My heart was breaking, but I couldn't let it show. I just had to be persuasive. I'd make him see this was what he wanted.

"I only mean that I like things the way they are, you know? I don't want to make things more difficult on you…or me. Ya know?"

I scooted forward in the bath, sliding my body in between his legs and turning to face the front of the tub, placing my feet next to his. I rested my head on his chest, and he wrapped his arms around me. "It wouldn't complicate anything," I assured him. "Babies are good. If anything, a baby will make things even better. Just imagine, holding a little one with my green eyes and your curly locks. And, oh, the cute outfits we could pick out." My body was all tingly just thinking about it. About a child growing inside of me, tiny baby kicks from inside my stomach. It was all I'd ever dreamed of. How could he not feel the same way? I wanted him to want it as badly as I did, to want to watch me grow with our child. To want to help me raise him or her. To want to love our baby as much as we loved each other. "Think about it: reading bedtime stories; trips to the park; family vacations; those cute little Christmas ornaments with their little hand-print." I closed my eyes, allowing myself to drift off into my daydream. "It's all I've ever wanted."

"It's really that important to you?" he asked, lowering his head so that his cheek rested near my ear.

"It's everything to me," I told him.

He sighed. "Well, how many are we talking? One or two, right? Not, like…six."

I snorted. "No, I had no plans for six."

He rested his head on the back of the tub and let out a loud sigh. "Whatever you want, my love, it's yours."

I grinned from ear to ear, pulling his arms tighter around me. "You really mean it?" I glanced over my shoulder at him.

He kissed my cheek. "My goal in life is to make you happy, Han. If a baby will do that…why would I say no?"

"Is it what you want, though?" I asked, instantly doubting why I was pressing the matter.

"What I want," he turned me sideways and brushed a piece of hair out of my face so he could see me clearly, "is for you to have the life you've always dreamed of."

I kissed his lips then, sliding an arm around him with a full grin. "I already do."

Like I'd hoped originally, we started trying then, right there in the bathtub. I just knew it would happen quickly —I'd always gotten what I wanted. I could practically see the child we'd bring into the world together. I counted down the days from our first unprotected encounter until the first moment I could possibly feel a pregnancy symptom. Every ache or pain, every wave of nausea, every yawn that escaped my throat pointed to the pregnancy I knew must be in progress. I researched heavily every early pregnancy symptom and searched for them with my every waking moment. I watched the calendar diligently, waiting impatiently for the day—the second—I could take the test.

When it finally came, I rushed into the bathroom with the box in hand. It had two tests—I had a very real picture of how I wanted to surprise Mark in my head. I couldn't wait to take a picture of my positive tests. When the first one came out negative, I convinced myself it was because it hadn't been first morning urine. I'd been hardly able to make it to the toilet, let alone open the impenetrable package that I needed to get into. So, when it came time for the second test, I waited with bated breath for the next day. I didn't allow myself to drink anything for a few hours before bed in hopes that I wouldn't dilute the urine.

But, despite all my efforts, the test result remained negative. Again and again I tested, waiting for that little pink plus sign, but it never came. Right on schedule, my period reared its ugly, red head.

The next month, it was much the same. I waited for the symptoms, begged my husband for intimacy at every opportunity, but still…negative. I was beginning to hate the way that blue line stared back at me so smugly, darkening as time passed. I wanted to be pregnant with every fiber of my being. I read pregnancy forums, searched for tips and tricks from fellow trying-to-conceive mothers, and waited eagerly for the first sign of my imminent pregnancy.

One day, Mark had come home from work late and was surprised to find me waiting up for him.

"It's late," he said. "What are you still doing up?"

I turned the volume down on the television. "Today's

my last potential ovulation day, so I thought we could give it one more shot."

He set his briefcase down and, with it, his shoulders slumped. "We just did it yesterday."

I raised a brow, feeling insulted. "Well, excuse me. I didn't realize it was such a chore."

"It's not a chore, Han. I'm just not in the mood tonight, okay?"

"Not in the mood?" I demanded, pulling my legs up under me on the couch. "How convenient is that? The last day that we have the chance and you couldn't care less about sex." I scoffed, rage fueling me.

"We are having sex more now that we've ever done before, and it's all because you want to have a baby. How do you think that makes me feel?"

I frowned. "All because *I* want to have a baby? You know, Mark, maybe we aren't getting pregnant because you're so against it."

"You're right. I willed my sperm not to impregnate you." He strode past me angrily and pulled open the fridge.

"That's right," I egged him on with fury in my veins. "Grab your wine. Grab your whiskey. Have yourself a drink, but God forbid you sleep with your wife."

He spun around with his back up against the cabinet, slamming the refrigerator door shut. "You're acting ridiculous, Hannah. I'm allowed to *not* want to have sex with you every once in a while. It's not a crime, you know."

I reeled back as if I'd been slapped. "Fine," I said, crossing my arms over my chest. "Just forget it."

"I didn't mean that," he said, the anger wiped from his face and replaced with frustration. "I'm sorry." He reached for my arm, stopping me from walking away. "I'm sorry, Han. I didn't mean that. I just...I've had a bad day, and I wanted to come home and relax, okay?"

"A bad day?" I asked. "Anything you want to talk about?"

He looked at me with a strange expression, as if he was actually going to open up, but quickly, his lips tightened into a thin line. "It's just...work stuff. I don't want to bore you. I just need a minute to wind down, okay?"

"Of course. It wasn't like I was planning to jump your bones the second you walked through the door," I said.

He smirked. "*Jump my bones?*"

"Yeah, you're acting like I was planning to force myself on you. I wasn't even going to bring it up, I just thought we were on the same page about wanting this to happen. It's been three months, and I'm starting to get worried."

"Lots of people spend months trying for babies. Three months really isn't that long."

"Sometimes I think you don't care about this at all," I said, my chin quivering as I realized I'd let my deepest fear slip off my tongue.

"About what?"

"About any of it, Mark. About having a baby with me."

"Why are you so obsessed with this?" he asked, slamming his hand down on the counter. "I'm doing all that you ask. I don't know what else you want me to do. I can't help it if you're not getting pregnant."

"I know you can't help it, but that doesn't mean you can't care about how I feel. I'm...I'm sad that it hasn't happened yet, and I feel really alone in that. It feels like you don't even think about it."

"It feels like it's *all* you think about," he said under his breath.

"What else am I supposed to think about? You've got me locked up here in this house all day. No job, no friends."

"Well that's a little dramatic," he said. "I've never told you you couldn't leave the house. Go see your friends, go take a yoga class. I don't care what you do. And as far as the job, plenty of women would love to *not have* to work. I would think you'd be a little more appreciative toward me for that."

I let out a breath. "I do appreciate you."

"Then maybe stop treating me like I'm such a shit husband just because I can't stay home and obsess over drinking beet juice to thicken your *whatever* lining and taking my temperature every morning just to make sure we have every chance of getting pregnant like you do. It's not my thing, Hannah. It'll happen when it happens, and I'm okay with that. I've got too much on my plate to worry about anything else."

I shook my head, taking a step back from him. "This is not how this is supposed to be."

"What's that supposed to mean?"

"Nothing. I'm just going to go to bed," I said, turning away from him. I waited for him to try and stop me, to reach out for my arm or call my name, but he never did. Instead, I heard the refrigerator door open and the familiar clinking of glass bottles as he wrestled the wine free from the door.

The next morning when I woke up, there was a box of red raspberry leaf tea on my nightstand with a note.

I'm sorry for fighting. It had been a long day, but I shouldn't have taken it out on you. I love you.
PS. This tea is supposed to help your whatever lining. ;)
It's going to happen this month, I can feel it.

CHAPTER TWELVE

HER

"Hey, girl," my mom said, pulling me into a quick hug. "You're losing weight." She stepped back, her hands still wrapped tightly around my biceps. "What's wrong?" She knew me too well.

"Nothing's wrong," I assured her.

"You don't eat when you're stressed, Hannah. Are you stressed? You look like you've dropped twenty pounds."

Thirty, actually, but I wasn't going to correct her. "Lots of free time. I've been working out."

"Well, don't lose any more. You're turning into skin and bones. I always envied your curves."

I changed the subject quickly, sitting down at the wrought iron table outside the café. "How are you and Dad? How's Henry?"

"Henry's spoiled rotten, as usual. If your dad doesn't stop loading him up with treats, the vet says he's going to end up with diabetes. Can you imagine? A cat with diabetes? Your father, though, he couldn't stand the idea of depriving him of anything." She smiled. "God love him."

The waiter approached us and took our drink orders, disappearing quickly after so the conversation could resume.

"You didn't order wine? My God, are you pregnant?" my mother asked, one brow raised. I couldn't fault her. Not a lunch between the two of us had gone by that I hadn't drank alcohol. And, to be fair, she had no idea that Mark and I had been trying, let alone struggling, to conceive. I felt my cheeks flush before I could answer and her eyes grew wide. "Oh my God, you are!"

"No," I corrected her, my hands thrown up to calm her down. "No, I'm not. I just…I wasn't planning to drink today."

She let out a sigh. "Suit yourself. So, what's new? How's my son-in-law?"

"He's well," I said. "Working hard. He's really loving his new firm."

"You don't look like you're loving it." God, she knew me too well.

"Well, he spends a lot of time there, you know? I just hope it won't always be that way."

She reached across the table and patted my hand. "You need to find yourself a hobby. Have you looked into a job here in Atlanta? Maybe I could get you on at the hospital. They found a place for me right away when I called about a transfer; I'm sure there'll be something."

Most people would hate the fact that their parents followed them across the country when they moved, but I wouldn't have had it any other way. My parents and I were close, and my mom had always been my best friend, so when Mark had proposed, the only thing preventing me was the fear of being halfway across the country from my parents. My mother is a surgeon and my father a writer, so it wasn't difficult for them to transfer to be near me, and nothing could've made me happier. Except maybe Mark being more on board with the whole arrangement.

My husband was charming when he wanted to be—he could win over anyone given just a few moments of their time—so I never understood his resistance toward my family. In the beginning, my parents were open and accepting of him, choosing to believe he was just taking a while to warm up to them, but eventually it became obvious that was not the case. Mark was civil when they were around, but it never went beyond that. He tolerated them, but he couldn't understand my need to be close to them. He thought it was odd that they'd traipse across the country to be near me and even more odd that I wouldn't protest it.

"Thanks, but no. Mark doesn't want me working right now, and—"

"Mark isn't the boss of you, Hannah. Don't let him control what you do. I could understand him asking you not to travel so much, that was a lot, but to ask you not to work all together—"

"I don't hate not working," I said. Then when she gave me a dubious look, I added, "Honestly, I don't. It's nice to have me-time. Taking care of the house, reading a novel every once in a while. Plus, I've been thinking of starting up yoga again. I haven't been able to do it since college, and I would love to get back into it. There are all these things I've never had the time to do before now, or that I haven't had the time to do in years. My life has been so busy since I started working, and I loved it—don't get me wrong—Mark just wants me to enjoy it more. He wants to take care of me, and I can't say I mind that." I was making that part up as I went on, but I at least hoped it was true of his intentions.

"So, what are you doing to enjoy it, then?" she challenged. "You said you wanted to start yoga back up. What's stopping you?"

I thought for a moment. What was I doing? Why wasn't I doing more? Truth be told, my days were spent obsessively cleaning our already clean home and reading passionate romance novels that only made me resent my husband more.

"Well, right now, I'm thinking of repainting the office…for a nursery."

My mother's eyes lit up. I wasn't sure why I'd said it, why I'd admitted it when it was the source of so much of my pain lately, but there it was. "I knew it."

I felt my face burn red and instinctively touched my cheeks. "I'm not pregnant. Not yet. But we've started trying."

"Oh, Hannah. I'm so happy for you, sweetheart." She reached across the table and stroked my cheek. "No wonder you've been distant lately…you must have so much on your mind."

"I do, actually," I told her. "We're…having trouble, Mom." She froze, dropping her hand as she waited for me to go on. "It's been four months and…nothing."

"You aren't overdoing it, are you? You know that can be as bad as not doing it at all. They say once or twice a week is plenty."

If my face wasn't red before, I knew it was then. "No, we aren't overdoing it." Hell, lately if I could get Mark in bed with me once a week I was lucky.

She pulled her purse from the chair next to her and placed it in her lap, pulling out her phone. "Would you like for me to get you an appointment with a fertility specialist at the hospital? At least you had the good sense to settle down in a city with decent healthcare."

"Do you think we should be worried?" I asked.

"I don't think it would hurt to make sure everything's working like it should. Four months isn't absurd, but at your age, it's long enough to get a second opinion."

I nodded. It was what I expected, but Mark's nonchalance had made me feel dramatic. "I'd like that," I said finally. "Thank you, Momma."

"Of course, sweetheart," she told me, running a thumb across her phone screen. "Think nothing of it. How's next week?"

"The sooner the better."

She placed her phone to her ear with a wink. "Consider it done."

CHAPTER THIRTEEN

HER

When Mark arrived home from work that day, I was waiting with dinner ready. He walked through the door with his head down, nose in his phone like usual, though the aroma of his favorite food seemed to catch his attention.

"Fajitas?" he asked, one brow raised.

"Mhm," I told him, stepping away from the table to take his jacket. "Here, let me help you."

He did so hesitantly, staring around the room as if he were expecting a booby trap. "What's going on?" he asked.

"What do you mean?"

"What's all this about? Are you wearing makeup?" He paused. "Are we celebrating?"

"Well, not exactly."

"What's going on, Hannah?" he asked. For some reason, whenever he called me by my full name, rather than the usual *Han,* I felt like I was being scolded. I walked his jacket across the room and hung it up on the rack before turning back around.

"I went to visit my mom today."

"And?" he asked. It irritated me, his lack of caring. No *oh, how is she?* Just one word.

"And I was telling her about us trying to conceive—"

He scowled and groaned, cutting me off. "Why would you do that? I hate the way you say that."

"Say what?"

"Trying to conceive."

"That's what we're doing, isn't it?"

He half-rolled his eyes, turning away from me and heading for the kitchen. "Yeah, it is, it just...I don't know. It sounds pretentious."

I scoffed. "Pretentious? Seriously? Are you just trying to pick a fight with me right now?"

He shook his head, sitting down at the table and beginning to load up his plate. To my surprise, he wasn't searching for anything to drink. "No, I'm not. Just forget it. What did your mother say?"

I sat down in front of him, taking in his expression. Try as I might, I couldn't read it. "She thinks it might be time for us to see a doctor."

He stood from his chair in one quick motion, the wooden legs roaring as they scraped against the tile. "No," he said, walking away from me as he began to pace. "You always do this."

"Do what?"

"You overanalyze and obsess over everything. It's been years since you lost weight, and you still count your calories to the single digit. When we went on vacation last summer, you spent two weeks checking destinations before we could choose. Sometimes it's like you get so focused on one thing, it's all you can see or think about. I'm sorry, I'm not going to go and see a doctor and get poked and prodded just because things aren't happening as fast as you'd like. Four months isn't that long. And, you know, if it's not happening right now, is that really the worst thing? You don't need to bring your mother into a decision that's entirely our own. It's none of her business."

"She wasn't making it her business, Mark. She was just trying to help." Fresh tears were in my eyes, but I couldn't bother to bat them away. "Why don't you just admit it?"

"Admit what?" he asked, his hand rubbing his forehead in frustration.

"Admit that you don't want a baby with me. You're only doing this because it's what I want."

He froze and dropped his hand. His eyes danced between mine. Finally, his shoulders fell. "Have I ever told you any different?"

I closed my eyes, covering my mouth with shaking fingers. "Your note did."

"It was what you needed to hear, Han. I wish I could be that guy. I do. I wish I could give you all that you want, but I can't. I'm not him. I'm not sure I'll ever be him."

"What are you saying, Mark? Do you not want to be with me anymore?"

"No, of course not. That's not what I'm saying at all. I love you, Hannah. I've...I've loved you from the first time I saw you. That night you walked into my bar, I'm pretty sure I loved you right then." He took a step toward me, his voice softer then, all of the anger gone. "But we never talked about kids. I guess I assumed because we didn't, we were on the same page. I see now that we aren't, and if kids are going to be a deal breaker for you, then I guess you have a decision to make. I want to be with you for the rest of my life, but I just don't see kids being part of that. I'm sorry. I should've been honest with you from the first time you brought it up, but letting you down is not something I enjoy doing. I wanted to get on board with it, I wanted to convince myself it was something I could learn to love, but I can't and it's not. Nothing has changed for me, and I never meant to mislead you, but I know you feel like I did."

"You were just so quick to want to marry me…I thought we wanted the same things."

"I know," he said.

"So, you're saying if we stay together…kids are off the table."

He gave a stiff nod. "I need to focus on my career. And our marriage. I just don't have time for anything else." His forehead wrinkled with concern as he stared at me, his eyes begging for an answer I couldn't give. An entire chunk of my future was being ripped from me before my very eyes, and the decision was ultimately mine. Mark or kids? Which meant more to me—my very real husband or my potential children?

"I just…I need some time," I said finally.

"I understand." He nodded, picking up my hand from the table. He placed his lips against my knuckle. "I love you."

"I love you, too," I said, more out of habit than

anything. With that, he picked up his plate and left the room, leaving me alone with my thoughts. As soon as he was out of earshot, I let my sobs consume me. It felt like a loss, and I needed to grieve the babies that had become very real to me.

CHAPTER FOURTEEN

HER

This is the part where you're going to judge me. Hate me. Up until now, Mark has been the obvious bad guy, but I'm not faultless in this and I'm willing to admit it. I was wrong. I was so very wrong.

Over the next few days, Mark and I spoke very little. He'd taken to working even later and sleeping on the couch, and we basically only saw each other in passing. I knew I had to make a decision about our marriage and my future, with or without him. It wasn't fair to keep either of us in limbo any longer than we had to be, but I couldn't make up my mind. Part of me wanted to admit that I'd never feel whole without children, that they were a part of my plan from the time I'd been old enough to hold a baby doll. That part wanted to leave. The other part of me loved Mark. That was the larger part, if I'm being honest. I guess I thought that eventually, once he felt more sure about his career, he'd change his mind, but I forced myself to think differently. I couldn't stay with the hope that he'd change his mind. He'd made himself clear. A life with my husband meant a life without kids. Was that something I could commit to? I wanted someone to tell me what to do, to tell me the right choice, but it was impossible. No matter what I did, someone was going to get hurt. In both scenarios, it was going to be me.

After a full two weeks of grieving and feeling numb, I walked into a yoga studio, clad in workout gear that had been packed in the back of my closet for years. I was trying to accept my new life, honestly I was. Yoga had once been a source of great peace for me, and I desperately needed peace.

"Hello." A woman behind a desk stood up, her hair tucked back in a tight bun. "First time here?"

I nodded.

"Welcome. I'm Shawna, the manager. What sort of yoga are you interested in? We have hot yoga in Studio B or beginners yoga in Studio D. A is empty right now, but there'll be a more advanced class in about an hour. There's also rage yoga in the back." She winked. "We have to keep that class separate from the rest. Also, we offer goat yoga twice a month on Saturdays. It's a ton of fun. So, what interests you?"

"Oh, um, well…probably just basic—"

"Beginners?" she offered, her voice too cheery.

"Yes, beginners. I've done yoga before, but it's been years."

"Beginners would be perfect, then. And if you get in there and decide it's too easy, you can just let us know. It's super easy to get you swapped. There are no fees or anything for that. Now, let's just go over some enrollment things quickly before the class starts." She led me to her desk and pulled out a packet, going over rates and hours before telling me the disclaimers and getting me to sign. I handed over the debit card as she pulled the money for a month's worth of classes and assured me I would love it there. I had no doubts about that. In what felt like another life, I had loved yoga more than just about anything.

I walked into the studio she directed me toward, pulling the yoga mat from my bag and finding a place near the back in the already crowded room. My gaze danced around the room, taking in the other women clad in their neon spandex. They were the kind of women I'd once been. Up before the sun comes up, workout in, fresh highlights, nails perfectly done. It was like looking into a mirror that took me back in time. As I stared in the *actual* mirror on the wall, I saw how my dark roots had grown out, quickly replacing the warm hazelnut color of my choosing. I saw the way the bags under my eyes weighed down my face and the way my cheeks, without a hint of blush, looked sallow and sickly. My nails hadn't been done in months and my yoga clothes were ill-fitting and faded. A younger version of myself would've been appalled at the way I'd let myself go in such a short time, but I couldn't bring this new version to care. I'd grown tired—of what, I wasn't exactly sure—exhaustion over-came me at the strangest times, and I found myself unable to care about anything anymore, myself included.

"Good morning, ladies!" A deep voice with a heavy Spanish accent carried across the room. I looked away from the mirror toward the doorway as a man entered.

No, man wasn't a good enough word. *God* was more like it. He was dressed in sweatpants and a tight T-shirt, the outline of his abs perfectly visible through the cotton. His complexion was enchantingly warm, as though he'd just come from a sunny vacation, and his dark, curly, and what looked to be chin-length hair was pulled back in a bun. I sat up straighter as he walked to the front of the class.

"I'm Luis. I will be your trainer for this morning." He pointed around the room with a twinkle in his eye. "I see a few familiar faces. I'm glad to see I haven't run you off yet, no?" He laughed and his laugh sparked a few other laughs throughout the room, all too cheery for my taste. It didn't take long for me to notice the effect Luis had on the women in my class. They hung on his every word, giggling senselessly at his jokes, and poking their butts out a bit more when he came behind them. It was infuriating how difficult it was for me to focus on the class with Luis there. He drifted past me a few times, his rich, woodsy-yet-floral scent surrounding me and making my brain foggy.

At the end of the class, my body burned with a familiarity that I'd missed. As everyone rolled up their mats, chugging water and heading from the room, I stayed behind, not yet ready to let the feeling go. My hair stuck to my forehead, slick with sweat, and I brushed it away, pulling out the messy ponytail and attempting to redo it.

"Your first class?" Luis asked from behind me. I jumped, spinning around to face him. I'd thought I was alone in the room.

"I, um," I was incredibly aware of the giant armpit stains I must be wielding, but I couldn't lower my arms as I wrapped the hair tie around my hair one last time,

"sorry. No, not my first class. My first class here, though."
I felt more heat rush to my cheeks, but I didn't see how
that was possible. "Have I lost my touch?"

He smirked. "Not at all, señorita. In fact, I was shocked
to learn that you were a new student. You don't need to be
in a beginner class. You could've been up there with me
teaching."

"Oh, I doubt that," I said, though in truth, I had taught
a few classes in college to pick up extra money. That
seemed like a lifetime ago. I was nowhere near what I
used to be.

"Will we see you again?"

"I think so," I told him. "I signed up for the full month.
I'll probably switch to a more advanced class after that,
once I get back in the swing of things."

"I'll be sorry to see you go," he said, his voice lower
than before. "I have a hot yoga class in the afternoons, if
you're looking for something a bit more
advanced...eventually."

I nodded. "Thanks...I may check it out."

He winked, his lips parting for just a moment as he
appeared to think. "I'd like that a lot." With that, he took a
drink of water from the bottle in his hand and turned
around. "Can I walk you out?"

I should've said no. I should've never gone back to that
studio, to that class. I should've walked away, but I didn't.
Instead, I heard myself saying, "Yes."

CHAPTER FIFTEEN

HER

I t wasn't planned. I never went back to Luis' class with
the intention of starting an affair.

At least, that's what I tell myself. I don't think it was a
conscious plan. But I was so lonely, I guess the thought
must've been there.

Either way, when the class was over the next day, he
approached me again. This time, I'd purposefully waited
around to be the last one to leave, in hopes that he would.
Would he notice the fact that I'd gotten my hair done the
day before? Mark hadn't. Or at least hadn't mentioned it.
Would he notice the waterproof mascara I'd carefully
applied? It was just enough so you couldn't tell whether I
was wearing any or I just had really great lashes. I'd
purchased new clothes that fit tighter on the thin hips my
marriage had given me. When I'd done it, none of it was
to impress Luis. I just wanted to feel better, prettier. I just
wanted to feel something.

"I'm glad to see you back," he said, running a quick
hand over my shoulder.

"I'm glad you're glad."

He smiled. "What'd you think of the class? Think you're ready to try something a little more advanced?"

"I think I like this one, for now," I said with a small smile. "But thanks."

"My pleasure." Something about the way the words rolled off his tongue had my stomach fluttering. "Hey, do you want to grab a coffee or something? I know a great little place across the street."

"Oh, um," I paused, probably for too long, and placed a hand on my stomach. His eyes followed them, looking for a ring I presumed. I hadn't worn one, of course. It was my chance to correct him, to set the record straight. I should've said, *"Sorry, I'm married."* I should've said no. Instead, I nodded, my voice caught in my throat. "Okay." His smile warmed me in places Mark had left cold for too long. "I'd like that." It was just coffee. I tried to reason with myself from the beginning that I wasn't doing anything wrong. I was allowed to have coffee.

But, try as I might to deny it, I knew what was going to happen. I knew based on the look in his eyes and the way his hand fell to my lower back as he ushered me out of the room.

I should've stopped it.

I should've said no.

I should've run away.

I didn't.

CHAPTER SIXTEEN

HER

"*Mi tesoro,*" he whispered in my ear, his hand cupping the back of my head as our bodies collided together. His breath was hot on my neck, our skin slick with sweat under his covers. He pulsed inside me once, twice, then exploded with a heavy groan, his body going rigid with release.

I was exhausted from our lovemaking, and yes, as pretentious as the word sounds, it was the best word to describe it. Luis was a patient lover, a man who made sure I finished first always, but he never seemed to tire of the process. He often told me he could've spent all day and night in bed with me, and believe me, there were days I wanted to do just that. But I couldn't, and I couldn't bring myself to tell him why.

He kissed my nose, sliding off of me and flopping onto the pillow beside my head.

"What does that mean?" I asked. I was learning so many new phrases from Luis. My knowledge of the

Spanish language was limited to two courses in college, and except for 'door' and 'cat,' I was basically useless.

He rested his arms under his head, smiling up at the ceiling confidently. "*Mi tesoro*," he repeated, drawing out the words on his lips. "My treasure."

My hands went to my lips instinctively, but he stopped them. He was learning my tells. "Don't do that. You *are* a treasure, Hannah. Don't doubt your worth."

I moved my hand to his chest instead, smiling in spite of myself. "You're incredible, you know that?"

He looked down at me. "Incredibly lucky."

"Say something else to me," I said, closing my eyes as guilt rose up in my throat in the form of bile.

"What would you like me to say?" he asked, running a finger across my bare arm and causing me to shiver.

"Anything." I wanted him to say that I was a horrible person. That I didn't deserve any of the kindness he was showing me. That I was selfish for stringing him along and keeping my secret from him.

He lowered himself so he was in my ear again, his stubble tickling my skin as he pulled me against him and sucked in a breath. "*Sólo puedo pensar en ti.*"

My body reacted to his words in ways no one had ever affected me before. I felt myself roll with excitement as his hand gripped my hips. I opened my eyes, waiting for him to translate.

"It means I can only think of you," he said, resting his forehead on mine. "And it's the truth. I know we've only been seeing each other a few weeks, but you're all I can think about, Hannah." He chuckled. "I think I'm going a bit crazy for you."

My eyes fell, and I closed them quickly to hide the shame I felt. Even during our greatest moments, the guilt of what I was doing never left me. I felt Mark with me everywhere. That's the thing about cheating on someone you love—and oh, yes, I loved Mark with everything I had —it doesn't *just* hurt them. Really, truly, my betrayal hurt me most of all. The weight of what I was doing, the guilt of it all ate away at me every day. I lived in a state of constant fear. I didn't know how people could do it long term.

"You shouldn't…" I sucked in a breath. "You shouldn't feel that way about me."

"Why do you say that, *mi tesoro?*"

I pressed my lips together. The truth was on the tip of my tongue, but I couldn't bring myself to say it. I couldn't bring myself to admit who I was or how horrible I'd let myself become. Instead, I did the worst thing I could possibly do in that moment. I leaned forward, pressing my lips to his and letting my secret become buried in the moment. It was selfish, but effective. Within moments, every care had faded and all I could think about was Luis. Luis' lips. Luis' hands. The way he smelled. The way he tasted. Luis. Luis. Luis.

CHAPTER SEVENTEEN

HER

W hen I arrived home that evening, Mark wasn't there. I'd rushed there from Luis' in an attempt to beat him home, so while I was relieved, it was surprising not to find his car in the drive. I hurried inside, placing my purse on the bench beside the door and pulling open the freezer. I needed to get dinner started, but I also needed to get in the shower.

I grabbed a frozen lasagna, not even leaving enough time for the oven to fully preheat before popping it in and rushing down the hall. The shower scalded my skin as I stepped into the stream of water, but I didn't have time to care.

I scrubbed my skin until it felt raw, as I did every time I came home from Luis', the pain only a piece of what I felt I deserved. I couldn't explain what made me keep going back to him, except that while I felt numb to almost everything in my life, Luis made me feel...something. Guilt, passion, anger, love...whatever it was, he was the first person who'd made me feel human in so long, and I couldn't stomach the thought of letting that go.

I finished my shower in record time and threw one towel around my hair and another around myself before shuffling down the hall toward the bedroom. I lifted the blind slightly to stare out into the drive. To my surprise, Mark's car still wasn't home. It was just past seven, and it wasn't like him not to call and at least warn me he was going to be late.

I stared out the window for a minute longer before pulling my pajamas on and running a brush through my hair. When I arrived in the kitchen, I checked the lasagna, which was only beginning to bubble slightly, and then pulled my phone from my purse near the door. There were no missed calls.

I went to my recent calls and clicked his name, watching the screen change as it began to dial. On the third ring, the call was sent to voicemail.

My heart began to pound as I stared at my phone in confusion. What on earth could be happening? I sent him a text.

Everything okay?

I watched for the bubbles to pop up on my screen, but they never came. Not sure whether to be angry or petrified, I paced the floor, staring at my phone with desperation.

Call me back. Call me back. Call me back. The mantra played over and over in my head, and every time I heard a car turn down our road, I practically leapt toward the window. Every horrible scenario played in my head: active shooter at work, affair, car accident, and mugging, to name a few. Maybe he'd lost his phone. Maybe he'd been kidnapped and held for ransom. Maybe he'd been murdered. Maybe he'd...found out about my affair. Maybe he was leaving me.

No. I'd been careful. There was no way he could've found out about Luis. I only went to his house when Mark was working, and I hadn't even given him my phone number or last name. We only saw each other in class—*class*.

Shoot. I'd given the studio my last name when I signed up. Was it possible they'd shared that with the instructor? Surely not. Wouldn't that be a violation of my privacy? I chewed my lip as I planned out my excuses. I would beg for Mark's forgiveness. Plead temporary insanity if I had to.

I made up my mind right then. If Mark came home to me, I'd never see Luis again.

AT HALF PAST ELEVEN, Mark still wasn't home and he hadn't answered my texts or phone calls, which were becoming more frequent by the hour. The lasagna was cooling, untouched, on the stovetop, and my salad beginning to wilt, but I couldn't bring myself to eat it without him.

I'd had enough. My body was filled with pure panic as I realized he may truly not be coming home. As a last resort, I walked out the front door and hurried toward my car, keys in hand. I didn't know where to look for him. If he wasn't at work, I had no idea where he might be.

I drove the streets between our house and his office quickly, checking my phone in a glance every few seconds. I pulled up in front of his office building twenty minutes later and stared into the high-rise. The windows of the building gave a clear view into the quiet, empty offices. Upstairs, I could see a few cleaners vacuuming and washing windows, but I didn't see Mark. I pulled into his parking garage and stopped at the gate. Without second guessing myself about him seeing the charge and wondering why I'd come there, I pulled out the credit card in my wallet and stuck it into the card reader, waiting a few moments as it processed.

The screen changed, and I took my foot off the brake but placed it back on instantly.

CARD DECLINED, the screen read. I swiped it again, with the same result.

"Excuse me," I said loudly, rapping my knuckles on the glass of the cage where the attendant sat. "Excuse me!"

The man, a hefty, older black man with a large mole on his cheek turned to me. "Can I help you?"

"I think there's something wrong with your card reader. It's saying my card is declined. I just need to get in here."

"I'm sorry, ma'am. Our garage is full of full-timers. You could try the one down the block," he said, preparing to shut the window.

"I don't need to park, I just need to see if my husband's car is here."

He opened the window again and furrowed his brow. "What do you mean?"

"My husband, Mark Oliver. He works in the building

across the street and parks here every day. I...I can't get ahold of him. He should be home by now, and I'm just, I need to find him. Please. I'm getting worried. It's not like him to be late."

The man's face filled with pity as he shook his head. "I'm sorry, ma'am, I wish I could help you. I really do, but I could get fired if I told you anything about our patrons. It's against policy."

"Can't you just break the rules this once?" I begged, feeling my voice choke up with hopelessness. "Please, I'm begging you. I just want to know that he's safe."

He looked around. "I...I can't." He huffed out a long, drawn out breath. "But, since you're already in here, I have to let the gate up for you so you can pull in and then back out to exit." He paused. "Now, if you were to pull through the parking garage and look for your husband's car...I'm not sure what I could do to stop you." His sly shrug gave me the first shred of hope I'd had in hours. "But...you make it quick, you hear? If you're gone more than ten minutes, I'll have to call the cops."

"I understand," I said. "Thank you! Thank you so much." As the gate lifted, I wiped my tears and sped in, zooming through the mostly empty garage in search of his car. When I reached the top, any sense of hope I'd momentarily felt was gone. There were a few cars in the garage, but no black Lexus. Mark wasn't there, so where was he?

I drove back down and out of the garage with a thankful but distracted wave to the attendant. Besides work, Mark's favorite place to be was home, so I had no idea where to look for him next. He wasn't one to go to the gym, his morning runs negated that need, so where else could he be?

A few moments later, I pulled into the parking lot of the bar where we'd first met. It was a long shot. To my knowledge, he hadn't been back there since he'd quit after graduation, but it was a last ditch attempt to find him, and it was the only place I could think of.

I walked into the darkness of the bar, the familiar smell hitting me at once. An odd mix of relief and horror filled me as I looked around, expecting to see him, only to find the place devoid of any faces I knew.

"You look lost. Can I help you?" A young waiter approached me cautiously, obviously trying to suss out if I was there to cause trouble.

I blinked myself from my trance and looked toward him. "S-sorry. I'm just…looking for my husband."

Pity filled his face as he followed my glance around the room. He thought he knew my story, but he had no idea. "Is he a regular here?"

"I don't…I don't think so. I, um, he used to work here. I thought maybe he'd…I don't know. I thought—hoped—I'd find him here."

The man furrowed his brow. "Used to work here? You don't mean Mark, do you?"

My eyes lit up and a smile grew wide on my cheeks. "Yes, Mark. Mark Oliver. Do you know him?"

He nodded. "Yeah, of course. We see Mark all the time. He's a good guy. We really miss him around here." He paused. "Oh wow, you're his wife. He wasn't lying about that. We were all starting to think he'd made you up." He smiled, his eyes making me uncomfortable as they trailed me up and down. "But no, I haven't seen him around here tonight. I just clocked in a few hours ago, though. Let me check with Vic." He hurried toward the bar, and I followed close behind him. "Vic, hey, this woman here is looking for Mark."

Vic was a busty brunette who wore way too much eyeliner and not enough of a top. She looked me up and down as I did the same to her. "Mark, what for?"

"I'm his wife," I said, trying to remain cordial. "And I can't get ahold of him."

Her stone-cold stare fell into something warmer. "He was here around five. Didn't stay long, though."

"Was he drinking?"

"Just a few, like always."

"Always?" I asked, staring at the waiter as he nodded knowingly. "What do you mean like always? Does Mark come here a lot?"

The two exchanged worried glances and she back-tracked her statement. "I, um, well...you know. Occasionally."

I knew well enough to know they were lying to me, and that Mark had been lying to me, too. My husband frequented his old hang out, drinking and carrying on, and hadn't told me a thing about it. As angry as I was at his betrayal, I knew it was no match for my own. Besides, the important thing was that Mark had been there that night but was no longer there. "So, you said he was here. He left around what time?"

"By six, I'd say," she answered, appearing relieved that I wasn't pushing for any more information.

"Thanks." I looked to the waiter. "Thank you both."

"No problem," he said. "I hope you find him."

With that, I was back out the door and into the parking lot. I sank into the driver's seat of my car and started the ignition. Where could my husband be? As I pulled out of the parking lot, I tried to decide which way Mark would've taken home. I remembered the way he'd driven me a few times after his shift, a street that would take us more of a concealed route, and on a gut instinct, I decided to go that direction.

The highway was quiet so late at night, and it gave me precious moments to think about all that had transpired throughout my evening. Being with Luis was basically a distant memory by then; all I could think about was getting my husband home to me.

What would I tell him when I eventually found him? Was I allowed to be mad that he'd stolen away to the bar and ignored my calls? Was I allowed to be mad that he was hiding his drinking from me? I didn't know. Truth be told, I didn't know anything at that moment. What I did know was that Mark's disappearance had awakened a fire inside of me. After Mark had told me that he didn't want children, I'd struggled to feel anything for him and I was worried that I might never feel anything for him again, but the events of that night had relieved that fear. My feelings for him were back as if by the flip of a switch. I loved Mark, and I needed to find him and fix our marriage.

As I turned around a sharp curve, my headlights shining over the tall tree trunks in the woods, I slammed on my brakes and gasped. The bright red reflection of my beams on his taillights nearly blinded me as I pulled over into the grass and fell from my car. My entire body shook as I rushed to him, taking in the horror of the scene in front of me.

There were tire marks on the pavement where he'd slammed on his brakes too late as he rounded the curve. The car had gone off the side of the road and slammed straight into a tree, the hood crumpling like an accordion. The woods around me were silent as I approached the car cautiously, looking for his body. *Please, God, let him be alive.*

I felt my way around the car in what seemed like slow motion, the scene playing out for me as if I were watching from afar. My fingers trailed across the black metal, onto the glass of the back windows, and finally to his shattered driver's window.

I let out a haggard breath as I realized he was still in the car. He hadn't been thrown through the windshield like I'd feared. Grasping the door handle, I pulled it open, reaching for him as a sob escaped my throat. Glass covered his body, and I dusted it away from his neck as my arm wrapped around it.

"Mark?" I asked, my own voice scaring me in the bitter silence. "Please…" His skin was cool, but not cold, though he didn't stir when I touched him. His neck was already bruising from the seatbelt, but as I slid my hand down his chest, my fingers now coated in blood, I let out a breath of relief. He was breathing.

"Mark," I said his name louder, reaching for the seat-belt as tears of adrenaline clouded my vision. I unbuckled him and clutched his face, his thick brows coated in blood from a head injury I couldn't see. Still, he didn't open his eyes. I let him go, feeling for my phone in an effort to call 911.

Without the seat belt to hold him up, he began to topple over, and I threw my hands out to keep him from falling out of the car. The sudden movement seemed to cause him to stir, and I heard him suck in a deeper breath. He was alive, even if only barely.

"Mark?" I cried louder. *Please.*

"Mmmhayue—" He made a noise that I couldn't replicate if I tried as his eyes began to open slowly.

"Mark?" I shouted at him, holding his head firmly between my hands. "Open your eyes, baby. Can you hear me? Can you hear me? It's me. It's Hannah." Tears blurred my vision, clinging to the ends of my lashes so each blink brought coolness to my skin. *Please just open your eyes. Please.*

His eyes opened once more, blinking as he tried to take in what he was seeing. The pain seemed to hit him all at once, and he doubled over, cursing loudly.

"It's okay, it's okay." I held him tight, trying to assess his injuries as he fought my grip in his arms. "You shouldn't move too much. I'm going to call for an ambulance."

"No," he said, his voice bursting from his chest in what sounded like anger. "No!"

"Hold still, Mark. I'm going to get you help, okay?" I spoke slowly to make sure he understood. "You were in a car accident. Can you hear me? Do you know who I am?"

He stopped struggling and stared up at me, his expression unreadable under the blood. "Yes, I know who you are, Hannah. God. Don't talk to me like I'm a fucking idiot." He shrugged me off of his shoulder, then grasped it and screamed in pain. "Just help me up. I don't need an ambulance."

"You're really hurt," I told him, unmoving. "You need to see a doctor."

He shook his head, rolling his eyes as if I was the one being ridiculous. He glanced back at his car, taking in the damage for the first time. "Goddammit."

"It can be fixed. I'm just glad you're alright," I told him, standing from where I'd been kneeling on the ground to help him up, despite my hesitations.

"*It can be fixed, I'm just glad you're alright,*" he mimicked in a high-pitched, sing-song voice.

I tried my hardest to ignore him, more worried about his behavior than angered by it. "But we should get you to a doctor to make sure of that. An ambulance will be the fastest—"

"*I don't want an ambulance,*" he screamed. "Do you have any idea how much money that will cost?"

I stared at him. My husband had never been one to care about money before, especially not since he started his new job. "I don't care about the money, Mark. I want to make sure you're okay."

"Of course you don't care about the money." He scoffed, lifting a finger to brush away the blood that was dripping into his eyes. "You wouldn't know the value of a dollar, would ya?"

"What are you talking about?" I stepped back.

He moved to walk away from me but staggered and stopped. "Whoa," he said loudly, one hand on his head. Then, to my surprise, he began to laugh.

"What are you laughing at?" I demanded, moving to his side. When he spun back around, he opened his mouth and spewed vomit in my direction. I jumped back, the bile narrowly missing me as he bent over and emptied his stomach onto the grass. "You've been drinking." I smelled the whiskey as soon as it hit the ground. From the looks of it, it was the only thing that had been in his stomach.

"Ding, ding, ding, we have a winner," he said, one finger in the air sarcastically as he stood and wiped his mouth. "Just take me home, will you?"

"What about your car?"

"I'll deal with it, okay? But not tonight."

"You don't want to go to the doctor? Even if I drive you?"

"I don't want anyone to see me like this, Han." The anger had faded away instantly, and his voice pleaded with me to understand. I was the only one who could see him at his worst and somehow, as sick as it sounds, that made all of it okay.

"Okay," I said with a nod. "Okay, let's get you home. Easy does it." I lifted his arm and placed it around my shoulders and led him toward my car. "Watch your head," I told him as I placed him in the seat.

"No seat belt." He held up a hand in protest as I tried to put it around him. "It hurts too much."

"Your seat belt probably saved your life. Besides that, it's on the opposite side. You have to wear it," I argued.

"*Just stop—*" he yelled. I let the belt go instantly, standing up and walking away. I couldn't allow him to upset me. I'd almost lost him, but he was okay. He was alive, and he wanted to come home with me. That was what mattered. That was all that mattered.

When I climbed into the car, I glanced over at him. He leaned his head onto my shoulder and kissed my arm. To my surprise, the seat belt was on after all. Seeing me notice it, he smiled up at me and gave a slight nod as if to say I'd won. As if to say, *anything for you.*

That felt like our agreement—as much pain as we'd caused each other, it was all for the sake of our love. Anything was possible as long as we had each other.

At least, that's what I thought.

CHAPTER EIGHTEEN

HER

I think I stayed up that entire night, just watching him breathe and making sure he didn't stop. When morning came, the sun shone through the curtains so I could get a better look at his face. We'd cleaned him up a little bit before bed, but I was curious to see what he would look like with all of the blood washed off.

He'd always been an early riser, so I knew when the sunlight hit his eyes he'd begin to stir. Sure enough, his eyes began to move beneath his swollen eyelids almost instantly. Within a few minutes, I was staring into his blue eyes, so bright in contrast to the redness surrounding them.

"Good morning," I whispered.

He nodded, adjusting his position in the bed. It seemed like even a yawn was causing him immense pain.

"I put some Aleve there for you, and some water." I motioned toward his nightstand. "How are you feeling?"

"Like shit," he admitted with a forced laugh. He reached up for the pills with a grimace and gulped them down before looking my way again. "I'm so sorry, Hannah. I don't know what I was thinking."

I hadn't known what the morning would bring—whether he would be mad at me or if he would be defensive. His apology shocked me, though, and I cocked my head to the side. "Sorry?"

"I know that's hardly enough to make up for what I put you through. I don't know how it must've felt last night to find me like that. I don't—I don't know what I was thinking," he said again.

"I'm just glad you're okay," I said, still shocked by his apology. "I was so scared."

"I'm sorry I put you through that. I never meant to—I never meant to cause you any pain. I never drink like that anymore. I don't know why I did it. I let myself get out of control; I let my bad day get to me and forgot about all my progress. I…I thought that was the end for me. Seeing that tree, heading straight for it, I never thought I'd see you again."

My eyes filled with tears at his words, thinking of all the potential pain I could've caused him and how stupid I'd been for even thinking of being with another man. I pushed myself from my chair and onto my knees at his bedside.

"I love you," I whispered, taking his hands in mine. "I love you so much. If I were to ever lose you…I don't know what I'd do."

He brought our hands to his lips and kissed my palm. "You won't ever lose me."

"I almost did."

"It takes more than an old car crash to tear us apart, sweetheart. I couldn't give you up that easily."

It was meant to be a joke, but his words brought the reality of what had happened back to me. Suddenly, I was in a state of panic. "You could've died, Mark. Or killed someone else. You...you broke the law." I was nearing hysterics as I began to let it out. "You could've gone to jail!"

"I'm fine. No one else was hurt. The car can be replaced." He put a hand to his temple. "I was an idiot, but I've learned my lesson. It'll never happen again."

"It can't," I told him. "You have to promise me. No more drinking. No more drinking and driving. I can't be put through this again."

"You won't. I'm done. Last night was a wake-up call, and I lived through it. I know I have to get sober again, for you and for us...if you still want to stay with me. Have you made a decision?"

Was that what this was about? Surely my husband wasn't crazy enough to crash his car and nearly die, just to get me to make up my mind about him? I pushed the thought from my head. No one was that crazy. "I love you, and I never want to lose you. That's all I know, and that's what's important."

He kissed my head, taking my answer for what it was. "I love you, too."

"You should really let me take you to the doctor, though. I'm worried about you."

He shook his head. "You don't have to worry about me. I'm fine." For show, he tried to sit up, but winced and stopped. "Sore, but fine. Honestly."

"What if you have a brain bleed?" I asked, to which he laughed.

"You've watched too much *Grey's Anatomy*. I don't have a brain bleed. I have sore ribs, a black eye, and a bruised ego. That's about it."

"But wouldn't you rather get checked out just in case? Your shoulder is really swollen."

"I'm fine, Hannah," he said angrily, but his eyes went soft the instant he'd done it. "I'm sorry. Look, the truth is, if we go to the doctor, they're going to want to know what happened, and I can't tell them that. If anyone finds out I was driving drunk, if I were to get arrested, I could lose my job. The partners don't want that kind of publicity, and I can't say that I blame them. This was, well, it's better off if we just fix the car, bandage me up, and pretend it never happened."

I could understand what he was saying, but it still felt foolish to disregard his health in such a casual manner. "How are you going to explain your injuries? They're going to notice."

"I'm going to call and say that I need the week off. I'll blame it on a family emergency. I have vacation time, and I can do what I need to from home. It's no big deal."

"Do you really think you'll have healed that much in a week? These look like they'll take months to disappear," I told him, running a finger along the bruise on his neck.

He pulled my hand away gently. "My guess is, it'll be a vast improvement. And if I have to take a bit more time off, I'm sure it's doable." He sighed. "I know it seems complicated, but trust me, it's the easiest way."

Nothing about his plan seemed easy, but I wasn't going

to argue. Instead, I nodded. "How about a shower, then? You look like death."

He smirked with one side of his mouth, a look that had once made me weak in the knees. "What a coincidence, I feel like death, too."

———

To Mark's credit, he was right about his injuries. Though they'd looked bad thanks to all the blood, once he was cleaned up, they weren't as devastating as I'd expected. He had a nasty bruise from the seatbelt, a gash across his nose, and another above his eyebrow. There were a few minor cuts across his face and hands from the glass, and his knees were bruised pretty badly from slamming into the dash. Other than that, he seemed to be in decent shape considering the condition of his car. I'd helped him through his shower, washing the places he couldn't move to reach and cautiously scrubbing his scalp. There were pieces of glass mixed into his hair, and one in particular managed to pierce the end of my finger.

Once he was out of the shower, I helped him dress and led him toward the kitchen. "You must be starving."

"Actually, just some toast would be great. The thought of food right now..." He shook his head.

"You're pretty hungover, aren't you?"

His nod was anything but happy. I led him toward the table, and once he'd set himself down, I sat across from him and took his hand. "Do you...think maybe it's time we saw someone? You haven't been to AA in months. You said rehab was what got you to stop the first time. What about something like that again?"

"I'm not bad enough to need rehab," he grumbled, rubbing his eye with the heel of his hand.

I gulped and looked him over carefully. "Mark, you probably totaled your car. You're lucky you aren't dead. How much worse could you get?"

"Worse," he said, closing his eyes. His tone sent chills down my spine.

"What do you mean?"

"In high school and most of my early years of college, I was…drunk all of the time. As in, I don't remember a time when I was sober. I haven't told you much about my past because I don't want you to look at me differently, but it's dark, Hannah. The things I've seen and done…they would terrify you."

I ran a quick hand over my exposed upper arm, wiping away goosebumps. "You can tell me anything. You know that."

He grumbled again and squeezed my hand in his. "I know you think that, but you don't know what you're saying. I've done horrible things. I wasn't who I am today."

It was almost as if he wanted to tell me, as if it was bubbling just below the surface. "I love you, Mark. I know exactly what I'm saying. Whatever you've done…whoever you were, all I care about is who you are now. We can fix this. We can get you the help that you need, but you have to be open to it. You have to admit you have a problem."

"I know I have a problem. I've never denied that," he said with a snap, pulling his hand from mine. "I told you that the very first night we met. I'm an alcoholic."

"Okay, but what makes you drink…is it a social thing? High school, college, and now your firm…those were all times you were surrounded by others."

"It's an *addiction.* That's why I drink. There doesn't have to be any other reason. When I was three years old, my dad handed me my first beer and told me to drink up, and I never stopped."

I gasped. I'd known his addiction started early, but I had no idea it was that young. "You were *three*?" My mouth gaped open in horror, but I couldn't bring myself to close it. How was that even possible? I felt tears brimming my eyes at the thought.

He nodded. "Most of my life, we had no running water, but we always had beer. My dad made sure of that. So, I had no choice but to drink it in the beginning. By the time I was old enough to know better, I was already hooked."

"I'm so sorry, Mark…" It was the only thing I could think to say, though it by no means covered all that I was feeling.

His eyes always went dark when he spoke of his past, and he'd never mentioned his family except to say that he didn't want them at our wedding, but I had no idea it was so bad. My mind filled with images of my husband as a toddler, a filthy little boy, drinking alcohol to stay alive. How could any parent be so cruel?

"It's okay. It was my life and there's nothing either of us can do about it now, but the fact is that you have to deal with the aftermath of the screwed-up person I've become because of it. The man you married isn't perfect, and I never will be. I hate that about me. I hate myself for it most days. I wish that wasn't the case, for your sake more than anything—"

"You can't blame yourself for what your father did."

"I don't blame myself for that, but I'm a grown man, Hannah. It's been years since any of those excuses were valid. I took responsibility for my actions when I went to rehab, I had everything under control for years, and then I let myself slip once. Then twice. And now...I can't seem to find my footing again."

"Let me help you," I begged. "Please. Let me help you find help however you want to find it. I want that for you. I want to get you back to stable ground."

He sighed. "I've been so terrified to tell you about all of the darkness because I didn't want you to look at me any differently."

"I will never stop loving you because of your past."

"You can't know that," he argued. "But I love you for saying it."

"What are you saying, Mark? What have you done that's so awful? If totaling a car is the worst—"

"It's not," he said with a heavy breath.

"Then what is it? What have you done that's so wrong?"

His eyes danced between mine for a moment, and he rubbed his forehead. "Nothing," he said finally. "I just... alcohol has made me do so many stupid things. It's caused me so many regrets, and I'm so terrified that losing you will be my biggest regret yet."

I reached for his hand again. "You aren't going to lose me."

He lifted our hands to his lips and kissed my knuckles. "I love you so much, Hannah."

Guilt filled my belly as I prepared my response. Now was the time to tell him. I'd done so much wrong, too. I'd made so many mistakes. I needed to tell him. I should tell him. But…I couldn't. "I love you, too."

CHAPTER NINETEEN

HER

Mark stayed home for the next two weeks to heal. He told his bosses that we were back in Seattle dealing with an urgent family issue. For the first time in months, he hardly talked about work. With each passing day, his bruises were fading and our relationship seemed to be growing stronger. It seemed like we were getting back to our old selves. Maybe even better. I couldn't remember a time when he was more doting or comforting. We sat on the couch for hours binge-watching mindless television shows, and in the evenings, we'd cook dinner together or order in and eat with no pressing matters to attend to. It reminded me so much of how things were in the beginning.

I should've known it couldn't last.

On one of the last nights before he was supposed to go back to work, he called to check on the car. When he walked back to where I was waiting in the living room, I knew he hadn't received good news.

"What'd they say?"

"Same old run around as usual. It's not done yet, and they don't know when it will be done. You'd think someone dropping twenty-five grand on repairs would be prioritized over the damn piece-of-crap minivan needing some tires changed, but apparently not."

"Well, that's not fair. Who's to say the minivan isn't for a mom who needs a reliable vehicle to get her kids to school?" It was the wrong thing to say, and I knew it the second I had.

He spun around to face me with anger in his expression. "So because she has kids she deserves more than I do? Damn it, Hannah, why does everything come back to kids for you?"

"I didn't mean that! I just meant that maybe the person in front of you has just as much of a need for her car to be fixed as you do."

"Why do you always have to argue with me? Why can't you just be on my side for *once* in your life?"

I let go of the coffee mug in my hands so that it was resting on the coffee table in front of me. "When am I not on your side, Mark? I wasn't trying to start an argument." I felt unsubstantiated tears fill my eyes. "I was just talking to you, trying to make you see reason."

"Oh, so now I'm unreasonable?"

"What is wrong with you? Things have been so good with us, and now it's like you're just trying to start a fight."

He sucked in a sharp breath. "Oh, stop crying, would you? I'm just in a pissy mood. Ignore me." He waved a hand as if that would silence the argument, but I was already upset.

"You can't just tell me to stop crying, Mark. You don't get to tell me how to feel!"

"Oh, *for fuck's sake,*" he said with a loud groan. Before I could decide what was going to happen next, he slammed his fist into the refrigerator door. I screamed as he cursed, wagging his hand in the air from the pain. His knuckles had burst open, and I watched as blood quickly rushed from the wounds.

"Are you okay?" I moved toward him, but he held out his hand.

"Don't touch me," he commanded as I neared.

"Don't touch you? What has gotten into you?"

"I just don't feel well, all right? Aren't I allowed to not feel well? Jesus. You're such a nag."

I stepped back as he moved toward the sink to grab a towel and wrap it around his hand. I reached for his hand, too. "Yeah? Well, you're such an ass." Gone were the days that I'd let him make me feel like I couldn't stand up for myself because of the mistakes with Luis. I'd never let him walk all over me before, and no matter how guilty I felt, I couldn't let it continue now.

He struggled halfheartedly against my care but eventually gave in. I wrapped the towel tighter around his hands and pulled him toward me. "We need to get the wounds cleaned up." Without a word, he followed me into the bathroom where I searched for antibiotic ointment and bandages.

"I'm fine," he said finally, turning on the water and wincing as the cold hit his wounds.

"You aren't fine," I told him. "You need to get those disinfected and bandaged properly before you end up with an infection." I searched through the cabinets aimlessly, looking for peroxide or rubbing alcohol to no avail. I wasn't surprised; it wasn't like those were regular items on my shopping list, but I thought surely we'd have some lying around.

I pulled the box of Bandaids and Neosporin from a drawer and placed them on the sink. "I could've sworn we had peroxide around here somewhere." I paused, trying to think.

"If you hadn't thrown out all of the alcohol, we could use that," he said angrily. "It has more uses than just drinking, you know."

"I do know that, but more than likely, you'd have drank it by now, anyway," I snapped back.

His eyes narrowed at me, but he didn't argue. Suddenly, it hit me. "Mouthwash." I turned toward the shelf where our mouthwash normally sat, and froze. "Where is the mouthwash?"

"We're out, I guess. I don't know."

I turned to look back at him, surprised by his nonchalant attitude and the fact that he was no longer looking at me. "I just bought some last week when we were at the store. Remember, you said we were out then?"

He furrowed his brow and pretended to think as disbelief sat in my belly. "That was longer ago than last week."

"I don't think so. It was after your accident..." I trailed off, staring down at his hands as they shook. It wasn't only the wounded hand that appeared to be shaking. "How did we go through an entire bottle of mouthwash in a week, Mark?"

"What exactly are you accusing me of?" he demanded, his face turning pale white from anger rather than fear.

"Your hands are shaking."

He glanced at them. "Yeah, so?"

"And I dumped out your alcohol the night after your accident. You haven't had a drink in two weeks, but your mood swings and shakiness make it seem like you're going through withdrawals right now." I knew my stuff. I'd done research to prepare myself for the worst of his withdrawals, but to my surprise, he'd hardly exhibited any symptoms. I had convinced myself that maybe he was right when he told me he hadn't let himself get too bad, but as I stared at him then, I knew I was wrong.

He frowned at me, though no words left his mouth. He was daring me to say it, and we both knew I was right.

"Have you been *drinking* our mouthwash because I dumped out your alcohol?" I asked, my voice barely above a whisper. I cocked my head to the side and stared at him, my heart racing as I hoped and prayed he would deny it and that I could believe him.

He closed his eyes, squeezing his hands into a fist as he inhaled. "Could you just please bandage my hands so we can move on?"

"Answer me!" I screamed, feeling as though I might pass out suddenly. I clutched my stomach. Maybe I was going to be sick.

"What do you want me to say, Hannah? That I'm pathetic? We both already know that. I can't help it, okay? I want to be able to, I really do, but I can't. I don't know what to do anymore." He covered his eyes with his fists as he began to openly sob. It was the first time I'd ever seen him cry, and I wasn't sure how to react. I stood still for a moment, angry and baffled. When he leaned to me for comfort, I let him fall into my arms and placed my hands around his shoulders.

I patted his back, whispering comforts into his ear, though I desperately needed to hear them myself. What was I going to do? I didn't want to deal with any of it anymore. My life no longer felt like my own. How had we gotten there? How had we spiraled to such a low in the small amount of time that had passed? Was I only just now seeing the man he truly was? How could I continue to put up with it—continue to live that way? Such a big part of me wanted to bolt, to run away and never look back, but a bigger part knew that wouldn't be fair. I had to stay because I'd made a promise to do just that. Over and over, I'd told him I'd be there for him no matter what. I had known about Mark's addiction when I agreed to marry him. I had made a vow to take care of him in sickness and health, and now I was ready to bolt at the slightest sign of trouble. I hated myself for even considering the option, but that didn't stop it from being there.

I could leave if I wanted to, I reminded myself. The option would always be there. When he went back to work, I could bolt.

Maybe I should have. In fact, I know now that I should have. If I could go back and tell myself anything, it would be to run. The second I had the chance, I should've run.

CHAPTER TWENTY

HER

Then came the first reason I couldn't run.

Two days after Mark went back to work, I came down with a stomach virus. For an entire two weeks, I was sick more than I was well. Mark had gone back to drinking. I could smell the alcohol on his breath when he came home in the evenings, but I was too sick to fight with him. Sometimes, I think he preferred it that way.

His car was still in the shop and he'd opted to use my car rather than get a rental because we were paying for the repairs out of pocket to keep from having to report the accident to insurance, so I couldn't get in to see a doctor. I thought it would eventually pass, but when the fever struck, I began to worry.

One morning, on his way out, I reached for his hand. "Could you call in?" I asked. "I need you to take me to the doctor."

"You're burning up," he said, touching my arm and then my forehead.

"My stomach is hurting so—" I clutched it as a cramp

took hold, pulling my knees into my chest. "I think something might be really wrong," I said finally when the pain had passed.

He kissed my forehead. "Could I make you an appointment for tonight? I already took two weeks off after the accident. I don't know if they'll be so understanding if I keep having to take off."

Before his sentence was finished, another cramp came and I curled up, sucking in an agonizing breath. "It really hurts," I whined.

"Do you want me to make you some tea?" he asked. "Is it your period, maybe? Do you need to poop?"

"Did you seriously just ask me if I need to poop?" I demanded, sitting up in bed carefully. "I've been throwing up for two weeks, and now I'm running a fever, Mark. I need to go to the doctor. It could be something serious. Besides that, it's not like it's *my* fault we don't have another car."

He groaned and looked up at the ceiling, and the fact that he rolled his eyes didn't get past me. When he looked back down, I met his eyes. I was pleading with him at that point, human to human. "Please," I cried. "I've never hurt like this. It feels like something is stabbing me in the stomach."

He stood from the edge of the bed and loosened his tie. "Okay," he said finally. "Yeah, okay. Come on, let's get you to the doctor."

I stopped myself from arguing further as I realized he was giving in. Within seconds, he'd bent down and thrown my arm over his shoulders, lifting my weight like a baby doll. "I need a jacket," I told him.

"It's not cold out—" He started to protest but stopped and grabbed one from the hall closet, tossing it over my chest carefully. I was in my pajamas, but I couldn't care less. I needed to get something done. Something was very wrong.

Within the hour, we arrived at the hospital. By that point, I was half out of it and every bump caused searing pain to shoot through me. I felt like I was either going to pass out or die at any moment, and truth be told, I would have been fine either way.

Mark had been quiet most of the way, and I suspected that he was angry with me, so in a strange way I hoped I did have something serious, just to prove that we weren't wasting our time.

We spent another hour in the waiting room, me doubled over in pain, him grumbling every time a nurse came out and called a name that wasn't mine. When I felt a sudden gush between my legs, I squirmed in my chair, my face pinkening.

"Mark?" I whispered his name.

He jerked his head in my direction. "What is it?"

"I think I'm bleeding," I said, staring down between my legs. Sure enough, within seconds, crimson had begun to seep through my blue-and-white plaid pajama pants. "Something's really wrong." I was shaking at that point, my hands pale white as they clasped onto the black, metal arms of the chair.

Mark looked down at me, then stood, rushing up to the window where a group of receptionists stood talking. "My wife is in serious pain. We've been waiting over an hour—"

"Sir, you should be seen very soon—"

"We will be seen now, unless you want a lawsuit on your hands. I am a lawyer, and my wife is cramping and bleeding in your lobby while you sit around and eat coffee cake." I watched as he slapped the plate of food from the woman's desk onto the floor. Normally, I'd be embarrassed by his outburst, but I could think of nothing but the pain as it continued to grow. "Do your damn job," he said, turning and walking back to me. "Come on." He lifted me up, and I felt another gush. I squeezed my legs together, looking back at the puddle of blood I'd left in my chair.

"Did they say we could go?"

"I'm not waiting for permission," he said firmly, leading me toward the double doors. Before we reached them, a nurse pushing a wheelchair opened them. She looked at her chart with a confused expression. "Charles McKenzie?" she asked.

"Nope," Mark said, popping the 'p.' "Hannah Oliver. Your next patient."

The nurse looked as though she was going to protest, but I watched her eyes travel to the apex of my thighs, where the bright red stain was growing larger by the minute. She nodded without another word and spun the chair around. A receptionist met us as we passed through the double doors and handed off a folder.

"Mrs. Oliver's chart," she told the nurse.

We were taken into a room in the main hallway, and the nurse put the brake on my wheelchair as she flipped through my chart. She pulled an iPad from the cart beside the bed and typed something into it, matching the folder to whatever she was looking at on her screen. "You're being seen today for stomach pain. It doesn't mention bleeding."

"It just started," Mark told her for me.

"Okay, let's get you up here so we can examine you. Can you help me?" she asked, looking at Mark.

He nodded, helping me stand from the chair. Together, they half-carried me to the bed. The paper crinkled under my weight as I slid onto it, thankful for some relief from the agony of holding my own head up. I collapsed on the pillow as a new cramp took over, ripping through my organs with a familiar intensity. With each new pain, I was sure it would be the one to end my life. How could anyone survive pain like this for long?

"Okay, Hannah. I'm Amanda. I'm going to take care of you...okay? How long have you been in pain?" the nurse asked.

"J-just...today, I think."

"She's been sick for a few days, but the pain seems to have started this morning. The bleeding just happened," Mark explained.

"Are you pregnant?" the nurse asked.

"No," I told her, gritting my teeth and pressing my heels into the bed with another pain. *Oh! Please make it stop.*

"We can get you on some pain medicine, but I'm going to want to do an ultrasound to see what's going on. Have you been diagnosed with endometriosis or polycystic ovarian syndrome?"

I shook my head.

"What about any history of fibroids?"

"No."

"Any history of ovarian or uterine cancer in your family?"

Cancer? I gasped. "No!"

"Okay, stay calm," she said. "Just covering all the bases. Let's get an ultrasound and see if we can figure out what's going on." She pulled a cart from the corner of the room and asked me to lift my shirt. I expected the gel that she squirted on my belly to be cold, but it surprised me by being almost hot.

She lowered my pants just a bit and placed a paper towel around the waistband so the gel wouldn't transfer onto them. Then, she placed the probe onto my skin and began to press down, her eyes focused on the computer screen that was giving us all a fuzzy view of what was going on inside of me.

I tried to make sense of what I was seeing, but try as I might, I couldn't make anything out. She moved from one side of my pelvis to the next and then toward the middle. Finally, she stopped.

"What is it?" I asked, my mind still reeling as I tried to recall if anyone I knew had been diagnosed with cancer.

"Excuse me for just a moment," she said, turning the screen off and walking from the room.

Left alone to assume the worst, Mark and I met each other's eyes. "What's going on?" I asked him.

He swallowed, his face pale. He moved toward my bedside, wiping the cool sweat from my brow. "I don't know, sweetheart. I'm so sorry I didn't bring you sooner."

"I wasn't in any pain sooner," I told him. "We thought it was just a bug. If it's…if it's something serious, you have to call my mom, okay? I can't call her. We'd end up sobbing on the phone," my voice broke at the thought, "and I wouldn't be able to tell her everything I needed to."

"Don't talk like that," he said. "It's going to be fine. *You're* going to be fine."

I wanted so badly to believe him, though judging by the look on his face, I wasn't the only one who couldn't. Several agonizing minutes later, the nurse returned with a doctor just behind her. "Hello, Hannah, I'm Doctor Fielding." He was a tall, balding man with a thick mustache. His smile was warm, though his eyes told me all I needed to know. I'd been right all along. There was definitely something wrong.

He washed his hands in the sink on the far side of the room before walking toward my bedside. Another cramp hit me, though less intense than before, and he grimaced, waiting for it to subside before lifting the ultrasound probe to my stomach.

He was silent as he stared at the screen, moving the probe over my skin, pressing down here and there and adjusting the settings on the screen. Finally, he set the probe down and turned the machine off. He clasped his hands in front of him and sighed. "When was your last menstrual period?"

"I, um, well, I had one last month. I have the exact dates on an app on my phone. Why?" I tried to think. My next one wasn't due yet.

"I'm so sorry to have to tell you this, Mrs. Oliver." No longer was I *Hannah*, the fun patient, but I'd become Mrs. Oliver, the patient he'd be delivering bad news to. I had cancer. I knew it the second she'd asked. I was dying. Six months to live at most. "It looks like you were about nine weeks pregnant when your body began to miscarry," he said, his words catching me by complete surprise. "It's very common not to know this early, but I know that doesn't make the loss any less painful."

"P-pregnant? I was pregnant?" I asked, looking to Mark in shock. His jaw hung open as he stared at the doctor. "But I had my period."

"You were. I'm so sorry. It looks like the pregnancy was lost, which has caused your cramping and bleeding. Bleeding in early pregnancy can sometimes be mistaken for a period." He paused, waiting for me to react, but I felt frozen in place. "You were early enough along that this likely won't require any intervention from us. You're in the beginning stages of passing the tissue. I'm going to do a quick exam to make sure your cervix is dilating on its own, but I'd say that it is with the pain that you're experiencing. We can give you some medicine to help with that pain, but other than that, we just have to let nature run its course. Who is your gynecologist?"

"Dr. Absher…" I said, not entirely listening to him as he drolled on. What mattered most was that I was pregnant. *Was* being the operative word. No longer. For weeks, I'd been carrying a child that I had no idea about. A child I'd wanted so badly it hurt.

"I'll have Amanda draw some blood from you today, and then we'll need to get you in to see Dr. Absher for some additional blood testing in a few days to make sure your levels are dropping like they should." He looked to Mark, who I guessed must look as shocked as I felt. "I know this must come as quite a surprise. We'll give you two a few minutes while I have Amanda go get some medicine and prepare for your exam. Are there any questions I can answer before I go?"

I shook my head, though I could make no words form. "No," Mark finally answered for us both. Without another word, the doctor backed out of the room, followed quickly by the nurse. When we were alone, the tears I'd been holding back finally escaped.

How could I have not known? What if I'd come to the doctor sooner? Would that have mattered? Could I have saved my child? Mark moved toward me, and though every part of me didn't want to let him see me fall apart, I couldn't hold it in. I fell into his arms, feeling his strong chin resting on my head. He rubbed my hair, both of us clinging to each other like we were the only things keeping each other alive. My tears soaked his shirt, and I heard his soothing whisper in my ears. He didn't try to tell me it was going to be okay; somehow I think we both knew it wasn't. Instead, he just held me and allowed me to fall apart in his arms, my chest screaming for relief from the tears that wouldn't stop coming. It seemed like the room was spinning, like I couldn't capture enough oxygen to sustain me any longer. How could I be grieving over the loss of someone I hadn't even known existed? How could one person hold so much grief? I was sure I was going to combust at any moment, tiny shreds of who I used to be falling to the floor.

The woman I once was, the woman Mark loved, died that day alongside my child. Thinking back, she seems like a stranger. Then again, I'm not entirely sure I've met the woman I've become either.

CHAPTER TWENTY-ONE

HER

M ark took me home with the doctor's okay. There was nothing to do at that point but wait for our child to pass. I say *our* child, which I realize is presumptuous. Luis and I began our affair almost twelve weeks to the day that I miscarried. The baby could've been his, but saying so at that point would've done nothing but cause us all unnecessary pain.

They gave me pain medicine to numb the physical torture that I was in, but that did nothing for the emotional pain, which was a fair bit worse. I lay in bed the rest of the day, unable to eat or drink. Mark stayed home, checking in on me every few minutes.

I heard him downstairs on the phone, and I knew he'd have to tell his bosses what had happened. Somehow, that embarrassed me even more. I didn't want anyone to know how I had failed at the very first step of motherhood. That my body had betrayed my deepest desire.

Did I blame Mark? Not at first, maybe. But the longer

I lay in that bed, with nothing to do but think and scroll through my phone researching causes of miscarriage, the anger began to set in. With how much stress I'd been in, how could I be expected to sustain a pregnancy? And the stress was all because of him. I could see that now.

When Mark came to check on me the last time, it was dark outside. He sank down on the bed behind my back, wrapping one arm around my waist. "Can I get you anything?"

"A divorce," I spat. I'd been rehearsing how I'd tell him, but when it escaped my throat, rather than relief, I felt only fear. What if he agreed?

My husband sucked in a breath, not moving his hand from my waist. "You don't mean that."

I wiped the tears from my cheeks, staring blankly at the wall. "Why aren't you more sad, Mark? Don't you care that your child died today?"

"I care, Han. Of course I do. But...I mean, we didn't know about it. It wasn't really like losing a child. I mean... you know what I mean."

"It could've been a child, though. Our child. We could be hearing its heartbeat today instead of preparing to flush it down the toilet if you'd—" I stopped, hiccupping through another sob.

"If I'd what?" he asked, his body tensing against mine.

I remained silent. I wanted to tell him all that was on my mind, how I blamed him for so much, but I couldn't do it. "Just forget it."

"No, just say it, Hannah." He pulled his hand from my waist but didn't leave the bed. I wanted to fight. I realized that as I lay there. I needed to fight with him. I needed to scream and yell and put the blame on anyone but myself. I needed to feel something besides the overwhelming grief I couldn't get past.

"This was your fault," I said finally, my voice barely above a whisper.

"My fault?" he demanded. "My fault? How the hell is any of this my fault?"

"If I hadn't been so stressed, we may not have lost the baby," I told him, rolling over and wiping my eyes. "But I had to deal with the wreck and all of your issues. Of course I lost it. How could I not?"

To my surprise, he didn't lose his temper like I'd expected him to. Instead, he stood from the bed. "Well, I'm so sorry if my problems affected you in any way."

"Well, they did." Why wasn't he fighting back? I needed one of our classic fights like I needed oxygen in that moment.

"Well, you know what, Hannah? If you want a divorce so badly, why don't you just go out and file for one? If I'm such a horrible husband." He took a step back. This wasn't the reaction I'd expected from him. Rather than feeling better from the release of anger, his reaction was only making me feel worse.

"Just go away," I said finally, rolling over away from him. I expected him to argue, but he didn't. He stayed still for a moment, and I listened to his steady breathing in the dark room. Then, a few minutes later, I heard the door swish against the carpet and his footsteps departing in retreat.

I closed my eyes, begging for sleep. Nothing mattered anymore. Not me. Not Mark. Not our marriage. Not our future. All I could see was darkness. Emptiness. I wanted to get away from him and myself, and never see either of us again.

CHAPTER TWENTY-TWO

HER

The next day, I passed the bloody mass that the doctors said would've been a baby if given seven more months. With its passing, the physical pain subsided. I took a shower, washing the sticky blood from my legs. I was numb to everything. I know it sounds crazy, but if you haven't experienced it, you can't judge. To me, that clot was my child, and my loss was every bit as real as a mother burying her five-year-old.

When I went downstairs, Mark was nowhere to be found. He hadn't come to bed that night, not that I blamed him. I suspected he'd gone to work, and a very small part of me was furious that he could just carry on as if nothing had happened. Then again, as far as he was concerned, nothing *had* happened. He'd gotten what he wanted. In fact, I guessed he'd be more upset if I'd told him we were expecting a child than at the news that we'd lost one.

I couldn't bring myself to feel much more than a twinge of anger at him, though. Most of my feelings were dulled by the incredible numbness I felt. The anger I felt most prominently was at myself. Had my sins caused this? Was I paying a penance for all that I'd done wrong? It felt like it. If I'd never been with Luis, if I'd never lied to Mark, maybe...

I stopped the thought before it could completely form, though I knew where it was going. I walked into the kitchen, looking around. He hadn't even bothered to do the dishes for me. In fact, it looked like he'd only added to the pile. I considered doing them. The doctors had said getting back to normal was the best way to begin moving on, but I didn't want to.

I didn't want to get back to this supposed normal. Our normal wasn't good, and hadn't been for months. Instead, I walked to the cabinet that I never opened. The cabinet I'd ignored for years in support of my husband's sobriety while he continued to stock it. I pulled down the first bottle, a half-empty bottle of whiskey, and grabbed a mug from the cabinet next to it.

I poured enough to be considered a shot at first, welcoming the once-familiar burn as it filled my throat before settling into my stomach. I continued like that, shot after blissful shot, until all pain—emotional and physical—had disappeared.

My head was resting on the table, and I had no idea if I'd fallen asleep or just zoned out, when a sharp knocking sounded at my front door. I jumped up, the buzz of alcohol causing the room to move in slow motion as I made my way toward the sound. I opened the door cautiously, closing one eye as the sun blinded me. When I saw who was waiting for me, I gasped.

"Luis?"

"Hannah, oh thank God. I was so worried." He clutched one hand to his chiseled chest in pure concern.

"What are you doing here?" I was trying hard to make my eyes focus on his face, though the alcohol was protesting every step of the way.

"I know I shouldn't be, but I was worried about you. I've seen you every weekday for two months, and now you've missed nearly a whole month of classes. I hope I'm not overstepping, but I thought we left things in a good place. If this was your way of dumping me, let me know and I'll leave, but I was worried about you. I wanted to make sure you were okay."

I shook my head, trying to clear my fuzzy vision. "I'm sorry. I, um, how did you say you—how did you find me? Find where I live?"

His beautiful cheeks flushed red, and he looked down, tucking a stray piece of hair behind his ear. "You never gave me your phone number, or even your last name, so I had no way to contact you at first. But then I was so worried. We do keep records at the studio in case of an emergency. I tried calling you, but I got no answer."

Truth be told, I had no idea where my phone was. I hadn't thought about it since I was in bed yesterday and using it for research. "I'm sorry. I've just…I've been going through some things."

"I understand," he said, his eyes warming as he cocked his head to the side and waited for me to let him in. "Anything I can help with?"

"I don't think so," I said, though my voice cracked as I answered.

"Oh, *mi tesoro*," he said, leaning forward as I began to stifle sobs. "What is it? What's wrong?"

"I—" I clutched my stomach, unable to bring myself to say the words. Where would I even begin? There was so much I needed to tell him, but instead, I let my cries be my voice. He held me, there in my doorway, as my sobs brought us both to our knees. He whispered to me in a language I didn't understand, yet somehow it soothed me. His kisses were loving, not passionate, as he placed them in my hair, clinging to me for dear life as I cried over a loss he didn't understand.

We sat there for what felt like hours, me shaking in his arms while he rocked me and whispered comforting words in my ear.

"Give me your pain, *mi tesoro*," he whispered, the first phrase I understood. "Give it all to me."

When I'd calmed slightly, he scooped me up in the threshold. "May I come in?" he whispered before stepping foot into the home he thought belonged only to me.

I nodded, unable to prepare him for the pain I would have to inflict when he realized the truth about the woman he thought he knew. He carried me into the entryway and then through to the living room. He sat down in the recliner Mark loved so much and continued to rock me. He didn't ask for any explanation, and yet, I felt like I owed him one. The tears fell as quickly as I wiped them. What would he say when I told him the reason for the tears?

"I'm sorry about this," I said finally, sitting up away from his chest.

"You don't have to be sorry. I wish I had been here sooner to hold you. No one should have to cry alone."

"Luis, I—I," I sucked in a deep breath. "I'm so sorry."

"What do you have to be sorry for, *mi tesoro*?" His eyes filled with worry and then understanding. "Ah, I see." The smile on his face was sad. "You were trying to let me down easy by not coming back to class."

"No," I said quickly. "No, it's not that."

"Then what is it, Hannah?" When he said my name, there was no anger, just confusion. I was so unused to anyone regarding me in such a kind manner that the truth spilled out of me before I'd meant for it to.

"I…I had a miscarriage."

To my surprise, his eyes began to glisten at my words, and he pulled me into him as he let out a haggard breath of his own. "Oh. Oh, *mi tesoro*, I'm so sorry. I'm so sorry." He kissed my head and wiped his eyes quickly. "When? When did you…"

"I found out yesterday."

He placed a hand on my stomach, whispering again in Spanish, "*Descansa en paz, hija mía.*"

"What does that mean?" I asked him, when the words stopped coming.

"It means, 'rest in peace, my child.' Fear not, my love, we will see our baby again." He smiled, and his comfort and hope broke my heart. I should've told him the truth, I should've been honest about my infidelity, but he was the first person to show me true kindness about my loss. The first person to act like my child was more than a mass of tissue. So, instead of doing the right thing, I nodded.

"Thank you."

"Are you in a lot of pain?" he asked, baring his teeth in a grimace.

"Not a lot," I said, "but some."

"Do you have chamomile tea? I used to make it for my mother during her special time. It helped. I'd love to make you some."

"You're too kind, Luis, but you don't have to do that. I'll be okay."

He rubbed his nose across my cheek, pressing his lips to my temple. "I know you will. You are *fuerte*, my love, *strong.* But even the strongest people need someone to take care of them from time to time. Let me strengthen you."

In that moment, there was nothing I wanted more than to let him hold me and make me tea and care about me for the rest of the day—the rest of my life. But it would've been selfish. I needed time to figure out what I was going to do, and stringing Luis along wouldn't help anyone.

"Luis, I—I'm sorry. I really think I need to deal with this alone."

"I understand," he said, kissing my hand. "But the offer stands. Your phone has my number on it now. You can call," he lifted my chin so I would meet his eyes, "anytime. I mean that."

I nodded, standing from his lap. When I did, I gasped at the red stain I'd left on his jeans. "I'm so sorry."

"For what?" He shrugged as he stood. "It is no big deal. This will come out." He pointed to the stain, then to his heart. "This, though, the stain you've left on my heart—" He pulled me into him and pressed his lips to mine. For just a moment, every bad thing in my life faded away, and I realized how much I needed him. "Well," he said as he pulled away, "I'm not sure there's anything that will take that away."

I smiled at him, looking down. I couldn't hold his eye for too long without feeling like I was going to break down again. "Thank you, Luis, for everything."

He walked toward the door and turned around one last time to see me as he exited. "I meant what I said. You call if you need me. I will take care of you, *mi tesoro*. Every chance I get. Every day that you'll let me."

I pulled him in for one more kiss before closing the door and watching him descend the stairs of our porch through the beveled glass. All I wanted to do was call him back and stay in his arms forever. But I didn't deserve that. I deserved nothing. Instead, I searched for the remainder of my drink.

I WASN'T sure if Mark would come home at all, but to my surprise, at half past five, I heard his keys jingling in the door and then his heavy footsteps headed across the hardwood floor in the living room. He stepped up the half-step into our kitchen, and I watched his eyes trail over me, wasted in my pajamas at the kitchen table.

He looked around the room, taking in the dishes I hadn't touched and the open liquor cabinet. I expected him to say something, but instead he grabbed a glass for himself and sat down in front of me, pouring a bit into his cup.

He drank it down without a word, his eyes locked on mine. It felt like a challenge, though I had no idea why. I filled my cup up again, taking another half-sip. I was surely going to have alcohol poisoning by the time I went to bed. I'd never drank so much in my life, but I couldn't bring myself to stop. It was no longer bringing me any joy, but it seemed to be the only thing I could manage to do.

He took another drink, this time filling his cup to the brim. I watched as he turned the cup up and chugged the whiskey down as if it were iced water on a hot day. Who was this monster of a man? I stared into his eyes only to see darkness. Maybe that's what he wanted me to see, I don't know. Maybe that's what he saw in me.

"Are you ever going to want kids with me?" I asked, the words leaving my throat before I'd meant for them to.

He sighed, running his palm over his face. "I don't know, Hannah. I don't know what you want me to say."

"I want you to *care* about how I feel."

"How would I know how you feel? You won't talk to me!" He slammed his fist onto the table.

"You aren't trying to talk. You want me to be okay and just move on from all of this, but I can't. I can't just pretend it didn't happen. I can't just pretend I don't want children. I can't just pretend it's something we can move on from."

"So, where does that leave us?" he asked, pouring himself a new drink. It was as if the alcohol didn't faze him. He didn't seem to be affected by it at all. How much could he drink before he had had too much? I was almost scared to know.

"If you don't want babies with me, someone else will."

His eyes narrowed at me. "Are you saying you'll leave me if I don't want children? An ultimatum? Is that really how far we've fallen?"

"I...I don't know."

"How fair is that, Hannah? What if I was infertile? What if I couldn't give you children?"

My jaw dropped open. "*Are* you?"

He jerked his head back a bit, his brows drawn down. "What kind of question is that? You were *just* pregnant, so you know I'm not. That's not the point. What if I was? Would you leave me then?"

"Of course not. That's different than you choosing not to."

"But it's still a choice, isn't it? I mean, look, I'm sorry we didn't have this conversation before we got married. I thought you knew where I stood because of how important my career was to me."

"Your career?" I scoffed, looking up at the ceiling. "What about my career, Mark? You made me quit—"

He scowled. "Oh, I didn't *make* you quit. I'm so sick of you playing the victim card with me. Your traveling got to be too much for *both* of us. We've been over this. I thought I was doing you a favor. I was trying to give you a break and let you be home. If you want to go back to work, by all means, go for it."

"You mean that?"

"Sure, whatever."

I nodded. "I guess I just have to think about things, then."

"About whether or not you're going to leave me?"

125

Again, he took a drink, though I was sure I'd heard his voice crack.

"Is that what you want?"

He reached for my hand, caressing it in his. "Of course not, Han. I want you—us. It's all I've ever wanted. I want to be better for you. I want us to go back to the people we used to be."

"What if we can't?" I asked.

"I'll make sure we can."

"You can't just say that—" My voice was barely above a whisper as I responded, shaking my head.

"I can and I do. You know, when I said my vows to you, I meant them. I'm starting to think you're just looking for a way out." He paused. "If that's the case, Han—"

"It's not the case. I just...this is a *big deal* to me, and I hate that you're acting like it shouldn't be. We aren't talking about hanging up the wrong color curtains or fixing something different than we planned for dinner. This is the rest of my life—my entire future—"

"*Our* entire future," he corrected. "At least, I thought it was."

"I just...need time." I pressed my lips together, begging him to understand.

His face grew stern with disbelief. "You're choosing fictional children that don't even exist yet over your very real, very here husband."

"You're choosing to let me walk away from us because of it. You won't even try—"

"And what happens when we try and it doesn't work?" he asked, cutting me off.

"We hadn't been trying for that long. We could see a doctor—"

"I don't mean *try* try. I mean…what happens when we have a baby and I'm no good at being his dad?"

The question sucked the words from my mouth, and I froze, staring at him. "Is that what you're worried about?" I asked after a moment.

"Hannah, you've seen me. I can't quit drinking, and it's not like I was given any kind of tutorial on how to be a parent. I have no memories of my mom at all, and my only memories of my dad are of him beating the hell out of me. What kind of parent do you think they could've possibly raised?"

"I can help you!"

He scooted his chair back away from me, his hands up in defense. "That's, no, you're missing the point. I don't trust myself to do a good job, and I won't accept anything less. No child deserves to grow up the way I did."

"But is that the real reason why you don't want kids? Because you don't think you'll be good at it, or because you truly don't want them?"

"What difference does it make?" he asked.

"Only one of those can be fixed…" I reached for his hand again, and to my surprise, he gave it to me.

"I don't want to fail."

"I won't let you."

"You can't promise that."

"I can. And I do."

His smile was small, but it was there, and it was the only thing I needed to see in that moment.

CHAPTER TWENTY-THREE

HER

At some point that night, once the whiskey was long gone, I passed out. I woke up as Mark carried me to our bed. He moved the covers back, placing me down gently and removing my house shoes. His touch was so gentle as he eased my pajama pants down.

I wondered if I'd bled through them again, and then I couldn't remember if I'd ever changed them after I'd bled through them the first time. Either way, I was sure there was dried blood on my pants, but I was too out of it to ask. His hands ran over my skin carefully, his thumbs sliding under the sides of my underwear as he pulled them off, too. I was self-conscious. It had been a month since I'd shaved and I was sure it must look like a crime scene in my pants. I tried to move my leg, but it hardly lifted.

"Shhh," he whispered, lowering his face between my thighs. I felt his tongue graze my skin, and a moan escaped my throat instinctually. What was he thinking? The doctor had said we had to wait two weeks before having sex to make sure my cervix had closed. We couldn't do this.

He seemed to have forgotten our instructions as he lifted my shirt above my breasts, his tongue dancing between my nipples. I tried to wiggle free, worried about the blood between my legs—the lights were off, but surely he knew I was still bleeding.

"Mark," I whispered, my words slurring as I tried to move.

"Shh," he said again, this time his words were sharp and his hands gripped my wrists, pinning them down. The proof of his excitement was growing harder by the second against my thigh. He freed his erection from the zipper of his pants, rubbing his hand against me to get me ready as he so often did.

I wasn't ready, though. I was terrified. Would it hurt? The memories of my recent pain were so vivid. Would I get an infection like I'd been warned about?

"We can't—"

"Shhh," he whispered again, squeezing my wrists harder. I swallowed, closing my eyes and willing the tension from my body. We needed this. Both of us. We needed to be together in every sense of the phrase, and maybe this was the first step of getting there.

"I love you," he said, his face shoved into the pillow beside my head. I tried to say it back, and maybe I did, but the next thing I remember, I was waking up.

CHAPTER TWENTY-FOUR

HER

D octor Fremont sat across from me, one tweed pant leg crossed over the other. He looked up from his yellow notepad, lowering the thin glasses from his nose and clearing his throat.

"So, Hannah, how about we start by you telling me why you think you're here?"

I looked at Mark, offering him a smile that I hoped wouldn't show the nervousness I felt. "Oh, um, well... same reason as most couples, I guess. We want our marriage to work, but we've had problems. We're hoping you can help us work through them."

He wrote something down then looked at Mark. "And, Mark, when Hannah says you've had problems, what do you think she means?"

He rubbed his hands together in his lap, picking at a callus on his palm. "Well, for one thing, I'm an alcoholic." He sniffled. "A *recovering* alcoholic. And...that's been an issue for us. Ya know, and there are other things."

"Like?" He pressed us to continue.

"Like, Hannah has a great relationship with her family, and I don't." He paused. "With my own, I mean. So that causes us a little strain. And then... well, Hannah wants children, and I don't know if I do. So," he laughed nervously, "we aren't going to be easy."

Doctor Fremont's smile was kind, and I felt my nerves calming already. "The most important thing is that you're here and willing to work on it. You've taken a big step coming here today."

Mark reached for my hand, not breaking eye contact with our doctor. "We'll do whatever it takes."

"Good. That's good. Now, let's go back and talk about the beginning of your relationship. Mark, what were your first impressions of Hannah?"

"I thought she was beautiful," he said. "Smart. Incredible. She...she had this presence about her, you know? Like, she had it all. I just...I had to get to know her. I can't explain it. I've never been drawn to anyone like I was drawn to her." He met my eyes then, and I couldn't help the blush that warmed my cheeks. He'd never told me any of that before.

"And, Hannah, what about your first impressions of Mark?"

"He was handsome. Charming. I remember thinking that when he talked to me, it seemed like he really cared. You know? Like he was one of those rare people who asks you a question because he genuinely wants to know the answer."

Doctor Fremont was jotting down notes as we spoke, though I wasn't sure we were saying anything of significance. What could he already tell about our relationship? Were we doomed to fail, or did he see hope in us?

"And tell me about your first date." He looked between us. I wasn't sure who he was asking, but Mark went ahead.

"It was the same night that we met."

"Well, that was fast. You two hit it off right away, then?"

"We did," I answered. "Everything about the beginning of our relationship was a whirlwind."

"A whirlwind," Doctor Fremont repeated my phrase. "Do you feel like it happened *too* fast?"

Mark looked to me, waiting for me to answer the question. I hesitated, but shook my head. "It didn't feel like it at the time."

"But now it does?"

"I've just…I've learned things now I wish I would've known before, you know?"

Doctor Fremont nodded, and I felt Mark loosen his grip on my hand. "What sort of things?"

"I don't know," I said quietly.

He pushed his glasses back on his nose and looked at his page. "The thing is, I can't help if you don't choose to both be open and honest in here. This is a safe space, a place where we can work through our issues. But we can't work through them if you don't admit that they're there."

"Well, you know, the alcohol for one thing—"

"You knew about that from the beginning—" Mark argued, dropping my hand instantly.

"Mark, let Hannah speak," Doctor Fremont corrected. I smiled at him but quickly tucked my chin to my chest.

"When we got married, Mark was sober. I did know he was an alcoholic, but I'd never seen what he was like when he drank."

"I see," Doctor Fremont said as he wrote something down. "So, Mark, you're no longer recovering?"

"I am. I just...struggle."

"How long had you been sober when you met Hannah?"

"Three years."

"And how long have you been sober as of today?"

He looked at his watch with a sigh. "Seven hours."

Doctor Fremont nodded slowly. "Are you attending meetings?"

"Not regularly, no."

"And do you have a sponsor?"

Mark shook his head. "We've lost contact."

"Are you recommitting to your sobriety, then? Have you made plans to start attending meetings and contact your sponsor?"

"Well, not exactly, but I know it's what I need to do. I just...I work long hours. It's hard for me to find the time to do it like I need to."

"Sometimes it's easier for us to find the excuses than to find the time," Doctor Fremont said, his tone caring but firm. To my surprise, Mark didn't argue. Instead, he nodded.

"Yeah, it is."

"So, I think that's step one, then, don't you? If alcohol is causing a problem, and you're both committed to fixing it, we need to all get on board with Mark's sobriety. Can you both commit to that? No alcohol in the house. Hannah?"

I nodded eagerly. "Oh, yes. Definitely."

"Great," he said, writing something down. "Sometimes it's important to remember that even the most daunting things can be broken down into smaller steps. Then smaller. Then even smaller. The first step to fixing dinner is walking to the kitchen; the first step to solving this particular problem is to both be on the same page about your goals."

As our sessions continued with Doctor Fremont, I'd learned he was big on steps and goals, some of which we completed, most of which we never got the chance.

If only I'd known the night I met Mark, the night I'd thought was the beginning of the rest of my life, was actually the night that began my downfall.

If only I'd never walked into that bar.

If only I'd never said yes to the man who I let ruin my life.

CHAPTER TWENTY-FIVE

HER

The beginning of the end came in the form of my husband coming home from work early one day. It was exactly three months after we'd started therapy and, for the first time in so long, it actually felt like we were getting back to being the people we once were.

One sentence changed everything.

"I've just been suspended." He said the words with panic in his eyes, but no alcohol on his breath. He'd been sober for twenty-two days, enough to break a habit, thanks to Doctor Fremont's advice and support.

"Suspended for what? What does that mean?" I asked.

He scoffed, looking down at the floor. "It's stupid. It'll blow over, but the partners just...they had to do it."

"What do you mean, Mark? What happened?"

"I was...well, it's this damn *me too* stuff, isn't it? People think just talking to someone of the opposite sex warrants a lawsuit nowadays, don't they? Everyone's so uptight about things." He brushed his foot along the floor as I let the words run over me, trying to decipher their meaning.

"What are you saying, Mark? Were you...I mean, is there a lawsuit against you?"

"No," he said quickly. "No, nothing like that. Bill and Lonnie are going to take care of it. Just some stupid girl looking for a payout."

"Who is she?" I demanded. "What is she accusing you of?" My blood ran cold as I waited for an answer.

"McKenna Logan," he said. "One of the interns."

I knew McKenna. At least, I'd heard him talk about her. She seemed to be one that was always helpful on his cases. What on earth could she have to gain by hurting him?

"What are you supposed to have done?" I asked, trying to get him to meet my eyes.

He shook his head with a scowl. "Nothing. It's stupid."

"Well, it's serious enough that they've suspended you," I argued. "Were you sleeping with her?" The mere thought sent my blood boiling.

He rolled his eyes. "God, no. Of course I wasn't. I can't believe you could ask me that."

"What else am I supposed to think? You won't tell me what she's accusing you of!"

"That's 'cause I don't know! Bill and Lonnie aren't even sure. She's been talking to Leilani, the junior partner. They're all supposed to be meeting to talk things through, but they had to suspend me in the meantime. They just said they know she's made some comments to the other interns about me coming on to her—which I haven't—and they're trying to get to the bottom of it before it becomes something bigger than it needs to be. Like I said, it's stupid. Not a big deal. They just figure with me out of the office, they can get her to open up about whatever she thinks I've *supposedly* done and then get her to confess it's not true. Rather than embarrass her in front of me."

"Why would she go and stir up something like this and risk her job?" I asked.

"Beats me," he said. "Poor girl's got nothing else to do, I guess. Probably has a little crush on me or something."

"You're sure that's all this is?"

He nodded, kissing my cheek. "I'm positive. They'll get it all sorted, and then I'll be back to work in a few days."

"But what about your clients?"

"I can still work from home, can't I?" He winked. "No one has to even know this is going on except for the higher-ups at the firm, and they've all signed non-disclosures."

"Lucky they have," I said. "This is the kind of thing that could ruin your career."

He shook his head, grabbing a danish from the plate on the counter and taking a bite. "Good thing I haven't done anything, then, isn't it? Besides, I know a pretty good lawyer if things get nasty."

I followed him down the hall as he turned to walk away. "I don't know how you can joke about this. It's serious, Mark. This girl could—"

"The partners are handling it, Han, honest. I probably wouldn't have even mentioned it to you if I didn't have to work from home for these next few days."

"It's going to be okay, then? You're sure?"

"Positive," he said. "I don't want you worrying about this, okay?"

"Mhm," I said, blinking heavily as I tried to process all I'd learned.

"Promise me?"

"I promise."

"Okay."

"Okay, then, come here," he said, pulling me to him playfully and running his hand up my shirt. "Working from home just means we have time for a few extra breaks."

WELL, as you can probably guess, I *did* worry about it. By that evening, I knew all there was to know about McKenna Logan. Party girl who attended UCLA before coming back home after college to settle down and start her career.

Her social media accounts were flooded with public photos of her in tiny outfits, funneling beer, and making out with anything that had a functioning mouth. As I scrolled through her pages, learning more about her—like the fact that she thought we should *do something about all the plastic waste,* and that *she would only ever dye her hair with henna again, obvi*—I became more and more annoyed.

This girl was the kind of girl who gave the rest of us a bad name. The girl who cried wolf over something stupid, probably just in search of a payday. Student loans from UCLA couldn't be cheap, and I couldn't find anything that pointed to her coming from money of her own. I'd seen at least three pictures that contained nip slips, and I could count the outfits she wore a bra with on one hand. Who was she kidding? There was no way my husband would've *needed* to come on to her. If he'd been interested, it was *obvi* he wouldn't have had to try too hard.

I hated her. I hated her as much as one human being could hate another. Though Mark swore things would work out, I couldn't help but worry about if they didn't. If he went to jail, or if we were sued for this. If he lost his job. Worse, if he lost his license.

He'd been petrified of what a DUI could do to him, but what could any form of sexual misconduct allegation do to him in this day and age? I knew how it worked. He'd be guilty before he even stepped foot in that courtroom.

Courtroom. As an avid rule follower, the thought sent chills down my spine. How had I gotten myself mixed up in a life like this? In a world where women are fighting to regain all the power, how could I ever hope to prove the man was right in this situation?

Each day that Mark wasn't called back to work, I became more anxious, though I seemed to be the only one. I'm not sure if he was trying to remain calm for my benefit, or if he truly believed it would all be okay, but I never saw him break character. If I hadn't known better, I would have thought it was just another day for him.

When a week had gone by and he still wasn't back to work, panic really began to set in. He assured me that everything was fine, but my gut knew better. It just didn't feel right.

We continued going to our sessions with Doctor Fremont, who seemed optimistic about our progress. Mark was back going to meetings, he had reconnected with his sponsor, and with Doctor Fremont's guidance, we'd begun to open a dialogue surrounding our difference of opinion about children.

At Mark's request, we'd left the details about what was happening with McKenna out of our sessions. While I thought they might be helpful to discuss with someone else, Mark assured me it would only make things worse. There were too many confidentiality issues involved in bringing something like that into therapy, he said, and like the fool I was then, I believed him.

Doctor Fremont had encouraged us to look at every chance to spend time together as an opportunity. Because of Mark's busy schedule, even mundane things like doing chores around the house and grocery shopping were supposed to be done together. Though Mark had been readily on board with each of our exercises from therapy, there was a day when I realized I was out of tampons and we needed milk, but Mark was in his office working.

It was the first time I'd shopped alone since our therapy started, and it felt oddly refreshing to have a moment alone. I'd been focusing so much on my time with Mark that I'd let myself forget about time without him.

I loved shopping throughout the week. It was something I'd never really gotten to do when I was working, and so since the decision to stay home was made, I'd discovered that grocery stores during the week felt like entirely different worlds than on the weekends.

It was much calmer, for one thing. I could browse through the aisles endlessly, checking Pinterest for recipes and reading the backs of shampoo bottles searching for the perfect one without anyone rushing me.

After I'd perused to my heart's content, spending a few extra minutes reading about which celebrities had sported baby bumps at the latest red carpet event, I went through the checkout and collected my things. I'd gotten a few extra things than planned, but dinners for the next week were set and I'd found a new mascara I'd been dying to try.

As I was loading the bags into my car, I tucked the receipt into the side of my purse and placed it into the front seat.

"Hannah?"

I spun around to find the source of the voice. I recognized the woman in front of me instantly, though she looked nothing like I expected her to. McKenna Logan was dressed in a navy hoodie and gray sweatpants, her hair was in a wild ponytail, and her usually made up face was bare and pale. The dark bags under her eyes spoke of many nights not sleeping.

"McKenna?" I asked, my tone full of venom. "What do you want?" How dare she come up to me in public? How dare she approach me? I searched her eyes for anger or vengeance, but I saw only pain. Her green eyes began to glisten as she stared at me.

"H-how are you?"

"How am I? Well, you've got a lot of nerve asking that considering what you're doing to my family." I shook my head. "You should really just go."

"What I'm doing to your family—" She stopped, then nodded. "You've stayed with him."

"Stayed with my husband? Of course I have."

"How could you? How could you stay with him after

what he's—" Her chin began to quiver and she placed her palm over it, stopping mid-sentence. Her eyes blinked rapidly as if she were going to pass out.

"After what, McKenna? What has he done?" I tried to keep my tone firm in defense of my husband, but without answers, I was still searching for the truth of what he was being accused of.

She stared at me with a furrowed brow and confused expression. "He hasn't told you?"

Suddenly, I felt like a child who'd been kept out of something very important. I was the only one out of this particular loop. "He told me some. Not all."

"Hannah, he…" More tears filled her eyes. I wanted so badly to hate her, to see through the charade I was sure she was putting on, but I couldn't. As I stared at her, I saw only truth and pain on her face. What had my husband done to cause her so much agony? "He raped me."

I stepped back, taking in a sharp breath. "No."

She stepped forward, reaching for my arm. "I'm so sorry, I just—"

"No," I said again, opening my door with shaking hands. No. No. No. No. No.

"Please just hear me out," she begged, but I climbed in the car without another word. I couldn't speak to her. Not about that. Not about Mark *doing* that.

I shut the door, unable to meet her eyes. It wasn't possible. Mark was happily married. He had no need to seek out other women anymore, certainly not by force. Did he have any idea what he was being accused of? And for what? What was she hoping to gain? A higher position? I doubted it, based on the fact that she was grocery shopping in sweats on a Wednesday afternoon. Money? That was the most likely answer. But why my husband? Why not one of the partners? Wouldn't they be the obvious target?

I drove home with tears filling my eyes as so many questions swam through my head. None of it made any sense, yet I wanted more than anything to believe my husband. I wanted him to be telling the truth. I wanted McKenna to be the liar in this story, for it to be that easy, but somehow I knew it wasn't. I saw the truth of her words in her eyes. She was either a fantastic actress, or my husband was lying to me. But *rape*? Why? Why now? Wasn't he happy with me? Was I not enough? The thought made me sick to my stomach.

His words echoed in my head as I pulled in the drive. *"Alcohol has made me do a lot of horrible things."* I shook my head, forcing the thought away, but it was quickly replaced by a vision of his hands around my wrists the night we'd drank together. But...he wasn't forcing me, was he? I mean, he was insistent, yes, but it wasn't like I'd outright said no. I was half out of it. Besides that, he was my *husband*. It wasn't like he had to ask true permission anymore.

When I got in the house, Mark was on the couch watching a basketball game. I couldn't bear to meet his eyes as I stalked past him and into the kitchen with my bags.

"You didn't tell me you were leaving this morning," he called after me.

"I didn't know I had to."

I heard the television mute and his weight adjusting on

the leather couch. "You don't *have to*, but I thought we might go together like last time."

I nodded, not looking his way. "Well, I just needed a few things."

"You were gone a while. Is everything okay?" he asked, leaning against the countertop and staring at me.

I looked up at him with a fake smile but quickly let it disappear. "I ran into McKenna at the store."

The color drained from his face in an instant. "What did she say to you? Did you talk to her?"

"She told me that you're being accused of raping her, Mark," I said. "Is that true?"

He scowled, throwing his hands in the air dramatically. "Of course not. No! She's...she's lying, Hannah. To get you mad at me. To tear us apart."

"Why?" I asked, finally stopping my hurried unloading of the bags. "Why would she do that?"

"To...to...I don't know! I don't know how her sick mind works."

I put one finger in the air. "I'm going to ask you this one time, Mark, and I swear to God, if you lie to me..." I took a deep breath. "Did you rape McKenna Logan?"

"Of course not," he said, his nostrils flaring with anger. "No."

"Have you ever raped anyone?"

"No!" he insisted, his face full of shock. "How can you ask me that? You know me. You know what I'm capable of."

"Then why is she lying? Were you having an affair with her?"

"No!" he screamed again, pounding his fist onto the

counter. "You can't be serious. You know I wouldn't do that. You know I'd never do anything to hurt you."

"You told me that alcohol has made you do bad things...maybe you'd been drinking and lost control—"

"No!" he bellowed, stepping toward me so he was towering over me. I stood my ground, allowing him to get so close our noses were almost touching. "If you believe I'm capable of that, then just leave, Hannah. Just...just fucking go!" He waved his hand toward the door. I hadn't planned to leave, but I felt my hand tighten over the keys in my jacket pocket. Without warning, I darted toward the door.

He grabbed hold of my hair before I'd even made it out of the kitchen, jerking me backward. I turned around, my palm on my scalp to ease the pain as I stared at him.

"What the hell?" I demanded. It was the first time he'd ever laid a hand on me in that way. It wasn't like he'd hit me, but I couldn't even justify his actions by saying that he'd been drinking. My husband was stone cold sober, and he'd grabbed my hair like I was his property.

"I'm sorry! I'm sorry!" His expression was panicked. "I don't know what—I'm sorry." He hung his head. "I just couldn't let you go."

"You're the one who told me to leave," I spat. "I can't believe you just did that." I pulled my hand away from my scalp to check for blood, though it felt dramatic even as I did it. My skin pulsed with pain, my head and face burning.

"I'm sorry, Hannah. I don't know what's wrong with me."

"Can you just...*can you go*, please? I need a minute." I

couldn't stand to look at him. I was brimming with fury, and the last thing I wanted to do was to keep talking to him.

"Please don't do this—"

"Just go, Mark."

"Whatever," he said, stomping from the room. "Fuck this, man." I heard his keys rattle and the front door slam before I released a breath I hadn't realized I was holding.

CHAPTER TWENTY-SIX

HER

Isn't it unfair that birds can choose to fly away from their surroundings at any given minute? That they can just…open their wings and fly away when they're in danger. Do you think birds pity us? We're so trapped and limited by our inability to leave on a whim. I think back to that line in *Forrest Gump*, about being a bird and flying away all the time, but especially when I start reliving that night.

If I could go back, I would've flown away. Wings or plane, it wouldn't have mattered. If I'd just flown away, maybe no one would be dead.

I paced through my house, trying desperately to decide what to do. I needed to find out the truth, and I cursed myself for driving away before McKenna could tell me. I wasn't ready to hear it then, perhaps, but I needed to now. I needed to know the truth, and I wasn't sure I'd ever be able to.

I needed to find a way to contact McKenna, but how? I had no idea where she would be, except that I suspected she wouldn't be working. On a hunch, I walked into Mark's home office. I sat down in his office chair and opened a top drawer. If only it were as simple as flipping through a Rolodex. Technology had helped us in so many ways, but hurt us in others. Suffice it to say, the top drawer contained only a few random pens and some sticky notes.

I gave the second drawer a tug and gasped. Liquor bottles, some empty and some full, filled the drawer. How long had he been hiding them from me? How long had I been in the dark about the secrets lying in my own house? Maybe he'd never been sober at all. Maybe he'd always been nothing but a liar.

I picked up two bottles, launching them at the wall with a growl. I watched as the green glass shattered and rained to the floor. I'd have to clean it up, but at least for the moment, it felt good to see them broken.

I opened his laptop next, entering the password he put on everything he used, and searching through his contacts. McKenna wasn't in there. Next, I checked his email and searched for her name. I found an email from her and opened it.

It was completely professional, though I searched for any kind of innuendo to no avail. If there was something going on between them, it wasn't made obvious in this email.

At the bottom, my eyes lit up. Under her name was her title, Legal Assistant, and her phone numbers, both office and cell. I grabbed a sticky note and wrote her cell down before closing out of his email and leaving the office, careful to step over the broken glass with care.

I'd clean it up later. I needed answers, and they couldn't wait.

My phone was in my purse on the bench in the entryway. I pulled it out and typed in her number, pressing it to my ear as it began to ring. When she answered, her voice was apprehensive.

"H-hello?"

"McKenna?"

"Who is this?" she asked.

"It's…it's Hannah Oliver."

"Oh," she said quietly, but didn't bother to go on any further.

"I'm sorry I blew you off at the store."

"I can't say I blame you."

"I want to hear what happened. Mark's telling me something different, but I want to hear your version."

"Why? So you can call me a liar again?"

"*Are* you lying?"

"Of course not," she said, her voice breaking already. "I don't understand how anyone could lie about something like this."

"Then tell me the truth, and I promise to hear you out."

"Does Mark know we're talking?" she asked.

"No, and he doesn't have to." She was quiet for a minute, and I had to check the screen to make sure she hadn't hung up on me. "You don't have to tell me, if you don't want, but maybe I can help you if I know the whole story."

"How could you help me?"

I sucked in a breath. "I don't know." Suddenly, I could

feel tears in my own eyes, though I hadn't anticipated their arrival.

"Hannah?" she whispered, and I pressed the phone to my ear harder. "Has he ever hurt you?"

"I don't know," I answered honestly. I heard her sniffle. "Were you two having an affair?"

I just knew she was going to say no, but when her actual answer came, it took my breath away. "We'd slept together once before. Over the summer. We were working late and…it just sort of happened. I'm sorry." She was crying already, and it made it hard to understand her words, but I knew what she said. Somehow, it didn't shock me as much as I'd expected. I gritted my teeth but didn't respond.

"Mark was always…he was nice to me. Most of the other lawyers at the firm ignore us. The interns, I mean. Except when they need us to run errands. But Mark would joke around with us, make us feel included. When he started asking me to stay late and help him with a few cases, I thought it was because he thought I was good at my job. Law fascinates me. I could never afford to go to law school; I'm already drowning in student debt, so being able to work for Lyman and Associates is the closest I've ever gotten to having a dream come true. I would never jeopardize that by forming a relationship with one of my bosses."

"But you did."

"I didn't. Honestly, it was one stupid night. We both agreed it was a mistake and it wouldn't happen again. I even went to Mr. Lyman and Mr. Greenberg to tell them. I didn't want it to ever come out and jeopardize anything for me, so I thought the best thing was to be upfront and honest. I'll be honest, though, I thought they might fire me."

I clenched my fist, wishing they would have. How could Mark have lied to me? How could he have betrayed me?

"It's been months since I've worked that closely with Mark," she went on. "Things were...awkward, at best. Then about a month ago, we were working together again and we had to leave the office to meet a client. I thought we were going to be able to get past it. I wasn't going to bring it up if he didn't, you know? But then at dinner he had a few drinks and he started making comments about me to the client. About what I was wearing and how good I smelled. It was so unprofessional, and I was mortified. Honestly, I just wanted to leave, but I tried to sit through it, tried to salvage all that he was wrecking. When we left, I wanted to yell at him. I wanted to tell him I was going to report him to his bosses. To tell him that I was going to sue him for sexual harassment if he didn't stop, but I couldn't. I knew if I started talking, I'd lose it. I needed to hold it together. He called me a slut, told me I knew I wanted him. The truth is...I have a past. I'm not perfect, but I've tried so hard to repair it since I graduated. I *didn't* want him. I wanted nothing to do with him after the way I'd seen him behave. He was trashed. I kept trying to take the keys, because I knew he didn't need to drive in his condition, and as much as I wanted to get far away from him, I didn't want him to get hurt." She sucked in a breathless cry. "I never thought he'd hurt me, though, you know? I took him back to the office and went inside to get my keys. It was only a little after four, so people should've still been there, but the office was empty. I went straight to my cubicle to get my stuff and he—he grabbed me. He pulled up my skirt and I, I just couldn't move. I froze. I should've fought back. I should've told him to stop, but... he's my boss, you know? It sounds silly, I guess, but I kept trying to convince myself it wasn't happening. Like, maybe he was grabbing my leg because I had something on it. I don't know. Even saying it out loud sounds stupid. But...it was over quickly." A bitter laugh escaped her throat. "At least I can say that about him, he wasted no time. It was kind of a blur, but I just keep...flashing back to it."

I wasn't sure what to say. I didn't want to picture my husband that way, wild and rabid. It hurt me to think of him with another woman at all, but to think of him like that...I don't think there's anything worse.

"Anyway, he left in a hurry. He told me nothing happened. I was crying on the floor, with my knees to my chest in front of my desk afterward, while he was buttoning his pants. I couldn't speak. I couldn't catch my breath, and he looked down at me and said 'nothing happened, quit crying.' Like I was a child who'd fallen down. Like I was being dramatic. Then, before he walked out of the door, he stopped and looked back at me one last time and said 'they won't believe you, if you tell anyone. They won't believe you because you've already told them we fucked.' And that was it. He left, and I cried on the floor until I couldn't cry anymore. Then, I got up and left. The next day, I tried to decide what to do...but I was so upset still. I wasn't sure I could work with him. I considered leaving, but how fair was that, you know? I'd worked so hard to get where I was. So, I told Lyman first. He suspended Mark for two weeks—"

"Yes, Mark's told me that's why he's off, but he told me the partners are handling it. What exactly's being done?"

She was quiet for a moment. "This was…this happened months ago, Hannah. He was suspended before, but Mark's been fired now. He's probably going to be arrested soon."

I was sure I had dropped the phone, though I could still feel the plastic case in my hand. "A-arrested?"

"He was off for two weeks while they investigated. Then he came back for a bit, while Lyman gave me the choice of how to handle it. I'm sorry, Hannah, I…I didn't mean to hurt you, but he has to pay for what he's done to me."

Suspended for two weeks several months ago. I tried to think back. *The car crash. The day he was so drunk he wrecked his car.* "He told me he called in those two weeks."

"No," she said softly. "He's a liar, Hannah. He fooled us all."

"And he's fired now?" I placed a hand to my chest, feeling the racing heartbeat beneath my fingertips.

"As of a week ago, yes—oh, hang on just a second." I heard a noise through the phone line and heard a click as she must've set it down. I wasn't really listening as I heard noises in the background, muffled and underwater. I sank down on the couch behind me, my knees hardly able to hold my weight anymore. What was I going to do?

"…Mark…" The sound of McKenna saying my husband's name brought me back to reality, and I pressed my ear into the phone. I could hear McKenna's voice, high-pitched and filled with fear. There was a man's voice, too, but I couldn't make it out. What had she set the phone on?

I put one finger in my opposite ear, willing the noises to become clearer. Just then, I heard a loud CRACK, a scream cut short, and a thud. Then, silence.

A few moments later, the door shut again, and I fell to the ground, one shaking hand over my mouth as tears filled my eyes.

McKenna never came back to the phone.

CHAPTER TWENTY-SEVEN

HER

After the initial shock wore off, I stood from the floor. I still wasn't sure what I heard, but I could venture a guess. I'd never heard a gunshot in real life, only on the movies, but this was as close as I could imagine.

She'd said Mark.

She'd said his name.

But was he really there?

Maybe she was just talking about him, I couldn't know. Was she even dead? I considered calling the police straight away, but all I wanted to do was get out of that house first. Before he made it home. I needed to get away.

I grabbed a suitcase from the closet, throwing things into it as quickly as I could pull them from the closet. Where was my phone charger? What shoes would I need? I couldn't move fast enough as I darted around the room, my body convulsing with adrenaline. I hurried across the hall to grab my toothbrush. Where would I go? My parents' house was the obvious choice, but did I want to bring them into this mess? They were innocent in all of this. What if it put them in danger? I would figure it all out when I was safe, but at that moment, I just needed to get as far away from my husband as possible.

I darted down the stairs with the tiny suitcase in hand and slipped on the shoes next to the door. There was so much I was leaving behind—my baby book, a collection of figurines that had been handed down from my grandmother—but I couldn't stop to worry. I had no idea where McKenna lived and, therefore, no idea how much time I had.

I grabbed my keys from the basket on the bench in the entryway and pulled open the front door.

"Going somewhere?" Mark stood in the doorway, whiskey bottle in his hand. I jumped back, trying to shield myself from him as he entered the house. My heart thudded so loudly I could hardly think as I watched his hands, searching for the gun. Would he have already gotten rid of it? Could he see my thoughts plain as day on my face? Was the guilt of all that I knew written in my expression? "What's that?" he asked, pointing to the bag in my hand. "You're really leaving?"

"I just…I'm going to my parents' for a few days. To clear my head."

"I don't want you to leave," he said, reaching for my arm.

I pulled out of his grasp. "Let go of me, Mark." My attitude seemed to set him off, and he stepped in front of the door, unmoving as I attempted to push him out of the way. My tears were futile, my hands tiring of pulling against his weight as I tried to move him. "Please," I begged. "Please let me go."

When he touched me, I couldn't help seeing his hands on McKenna's body, holding her down. I curled my lip, shoving forward with one last attempt. He grabbed hold of me, lifting me and taking me into the living room. He sat down on the couch with me on his lap, his jaw tight. "Sit still," he instructed, fighting against me.

"Let me go, let me go, let me go!" I screamed, no longer caring about pretenses. I needed to get out before he killed me. It was me or him, and I had a feeling only one of us would walk out of that room alive.

His arms tightened around me until I could hardly lift my upper arms, making all attempts to get away useless. "This is pathetic, Hannah. Stop it. You aren't leaving."

I opened my mouth, letting out a guttural scream until he clamped his hand over my mouth, pressing in so hard I was sure my teeth were going to break off. I tasted my own blood from the pressure. He spoke through gritted teeth.

"Shut the hell up before someone calls the police."

"You'd know all about that, wouldn't you?" I sneered as he removed his hand, wriggling my shoulders again to try and escape his grasp.

"Excuse me?" he demanded, turning me around so quickly I fell from his lap. I landed on the hardwood with a thud, my shoulder taking the brunt of the fall.

I scooted across the floor as fast as I could, trying to stand up. He was quicker, though, lifting me up once again. He squeezed my body in a forceful hug until I cried out.

"Stop trying to leave. Why are you doing this?" he asked. "Why are you making me this way?"

"I just want to go," I told him, hanging my head down. He pressed his forehead into mine so hard I was sure I'd have a bruise.

"I can't be without you, don't you get that?"

"Just...kill me if you're going to kill me," I cried, my whole body stiff in his arms.

His grip loosened slightly, and he looked at me as if I was going insane. "What are you talking about? I'm not going to kill you, Hannah. You're my wife. I love you."

"You have a funny way of showing it," I spat. "You don't hurt the people you love."

"I don't want to hurt you. I just want you to stay with me so we can talk this through. Things are stressful right now, I know, but we love each other, don't we? We can figure this out."

"Fine," I said.

His face was panicked as he stared at me, our eyes locked together. "Fine?" he asked. "You'll stay?"

"You aren't giving me a choice."

"You're being irrational," he said. "You're upset, I get it. I would be, too. But you can't just walk away from me. Not because of this. Not because of her."

I felt as though I was going to be sick at the careless way he could bring her up. "What did you do to her, Mark?" I'm not sure why I asked. I already knew, and I suspected what his response would be, but the question was out of my mouth before I could stop it.

His blue eyes—eyes I'd loved and looked into so many times before—grew dark, the creases around them becoming more defined. I watched his hand rise, the long fingers I'd held at the altar not so long ago balling into a fist. I saw the blow coming, but there was nothing I could do to stop it.

Waiting.

Waiting.

Waiting.

THWACK.

Darkness.

CHAPTER TWENTY-EIGHT

HER

When I came to, I was lying on our bed in the darkness. I lay as still as possible, not daring to breathe too loudly. I listened carefully for him to make a sound, knowing he must be lying in wait somewhere.

After a moment, I moved my hand across the comforter toward his side of the bed, a few inches every ten seconds or so. I waited for my fingertips to feel the covers rising to cover his body, but he wasn't there. With bated breath, I turned my head ever so slightly, looking toward his side of the room. When I was sure he wasn't in bed with me, I looked to the other side.

The room was eerily silent except for the sound of my own heartbeat. I waited.

Waited.

Waited.

Waited.

Nothing. If he was there, he was being incredibly silent. I reached my hands across the room and toward the nightstand where my phone should be. If I could find it, I could call 911 and wait for their rescue in the solace of my bedroom.

Of course, as evil as I was discovering my husband was, I could never accuse him of being stupid. My hand fumbled across the bare nightstand, connecting only with the lamp.

With no other choice, I sat up in bed, sliding my feet out from under the covers with trepidation. I pictured him launching out from under the bed, grabbing my feet like some wild boogeyman, but to my relief, they connected with the carpet without incident, and I stood, my head ringing slightly. I pressed my fingers to my temple, jerking my head back when they connected with what I assumed would be a huge bruise in the light of day.

I looked around the dark room, considering my options. I could pretend to stay asleep, but that would eventually do me no good. I couldn't sleep forever, and who knew what Mark had planned. Would my fate be the same as McKenna's? I couldn't try to escape out our third story bedroom window, so without a phone, I didn't see many choices. I walked across the bedroom, careful not to let my footsteps make any noise. When my outstretched hands met the door, I swallowed, preparing myself for whatever may lay outside that door. I wouldn't go down without a fight, I promised myself that. If this was how it ended, I hoped and prayed he'd get rid of my body so my parents wouldn't have to see what had become of me.

I opened the door swiftly, stepping out into the hall. I looked right, then left, letting out a relieved breath when I saw no one. I pressed my body against the wall, sliding carefully down until I reached the staircase. I looked across the main floor, searching for him. A man I'd loved, who I was now sure wanted to kill me. If it came down to it, me or him, would I be able to make the decision? End his life if it meant saving mine? I wasn't sure. I didn't even want to think about it.

I could hear something.

Rubbing.

Scrubbing.

I closed my eyes, listening closely. The sound was coming from my right. If I had to guess, I believed my husband was in the living room. I heard the clamor of glass bottles. Another guess, he was drinking.

Suddenly, I had an idea. It was a long shot, but it could work.

I hurried back down the hall, keeping my footsteps quiet. When I reached the bathroom, I darted across the linoleum, flipping on the dim light above the sink and opening the cabinets.

Where was it? Where was it? I searched for the purple bottle, praying I hadn't thrown it away during the move. Just as I was about to give up hope, I spotted it.

The small, purple bottle sat on the top shelf, behind my menstrual relief medicine. I turned it around, reading the label: **Take one tablet before bed as needed to induce sleep.**

During my years as a pharmaceutical rep, just one pill would knock me out for an eight-hour flight. In the beginning, it had been hard for me to sleep with so many distractions, and there were days when the flight was my only chance for sleep. After a while, I learned to sleep without the pills, but I always kept a few on hand for particularly noisy flights.

I twisted off the cap, refusing to let myself think about what I was doing. I had to get myself out of that house. I had to get the police to McKenna. This had to end.

I poured the remaining four pills out of the bottle and placed it back where it had been. I shut the cabinet and picked up the metal soap dispenser, pressing it into the pills until they split, sending powder everywhere. I swept the medicine into my palm and flipped off the light, hurrying down the hall again.

This time, I turned left and rushed into his office. I opened the second drawer quickly, pulling out a half-empty bottle of whiskey. I took a deep breath and lifted my palm to the bottle, dropping the white powder into the drink. I lifted the bottle so it was eye level and swirled it around, watching as the medicine dissolved. There was a tiny bit of white left fizzing to the top, but I doubted very much that he would notice it. Not in his current state.

I pressed my ear to the office door, listening to be sure I didn't hear him before I opened it. The next step was the scariest, but it had to be done. I went to the back set of stairs that led directly to our kitchen. They were extremely narrow and noisy and we preferred not to use them, but in this instance I had no other choice. I tiptoed down them, pressing my foot into each step carefully to ease the squeaks. I could still hear him in the living room, and I stopped at the edge of the kitchen before passing through the doorway. I could see him, his back to me, on his hands and knees. He was scrubbing the floor, and I was immediately overwhelmed by the smell of bleach. *He was cleaning up my blood.* I realized it in an instant, and I wondered just how much of a mess I'd made for him. From the way my head throbbed, I'd say quite a bit.

I placed the bottle on the counter, opening the cabinet to see what he had left. I pulled a full bottle down and dumped it down the drain, making the liquid splash against the side of the sink so it wouldn't make too much noise. When I was done, I placed it in the trashcan and started to put the tainted bottle in its place. I just had to hope my husband made it through the bottle he was drinking and to this one before the night was over. If I knew him at all, he would.

"What are you doing?"

I spun around, nearly dropping the bottle to the ground, but I managed to catch it. I flinched at the sight of my husband. Our eyes locked together, and it was clear we were at a standoff. Which of us would budge first?

The idea came to me as fast as it left my mouth, and I was flying by the seat of my pants as I went. "Oh, Mark, are you okay?" I darted toward him, reaching for his blood-soaked shirt. "What happened?"

He cocked his head to the side. "What do you mean?"

"Are you hurt? Where did this blood come from?" I tried my damndest to look innocent, but I'm pretty sure his buzz was the only thing making it work.

"I, um," he scratched the back of his neck, "you don't remember?"

I shook my head. "Remember what?"

"You, um, fell earlier," he said. He wasn't even trying to make it convincing, the lie clearly forming in his head as he spoke. "On the ground. Hit your head. Bled a lot. It was bad."

"Oh," I said, touching a place that wasn't hurting before I bumped the wound on my head. "Ouch. Yes, I guess I did. Well, no wonder I have such a headache. I don't remember a thing. Is it bad?" I moved to the left, unwilling to turn my back on him, and glanced at my reflection in the toaster. "Yikes. Should we go to the hospital?"

"Head wounds just bleed a lot," he said. "You'll be fine."

What limited knowledge he had of anything medical I was sure he'd gotten from reruns of *House*, but I nodded anyway. "Okay, good. Thank you for…for taking care of me. I was…going to pour myself a glass. Do you want some?"

"Sure," he said, eyeing the bottle suspiciously. I was afraid I'd been caught, but he was at least giving me the benefit of the doubt. He made no mention of the alcohol that was undoubtedly sitting in the living room waiting on him as he took the bottle from me. He lifted it to the light and stared at it for a moment before sniffing it.

I forced a giggle. "What are you doing?"

He shoved it toward me. "You first."

"What do you think I've done to it?" I asked, my lips pressed in a line as I faked a dubious look. He didn't answer but pushed the bottle toward me again. "I-I don't know. With my head, maybe I shouldn't be drinking."

"Drink it," he said again, and I saw the vein in his neck throb, causing my lips to quiver. With a whimper, I put the bottle to my lips and chugged, hoping it would be enough to end it all. It burned as it went down and I choked and chortled, but I didn't stop drinking until the bottle was jerked from my grasp. Much to my dismay, I'd barely made a dent in the amount that I'd left for him. It felt like I'd almost had it gone.

He lifted the bottle to his lips, staring at me out of the corner of his eyes as he drank. When he lowered it, he licked his lips. After a moment, he took another swig. Within minutes, the remainder of the liquid was gone. I watched his movements, waiting to see if he'd grow tired quickly.

As the room began to grow hazy, my eyes feeling heavy, I let out a troubled yawn. It was as if I'd managed to get all of the pills in my teaspoon of alcohol, while my husband had a fourth of the bottle and didn't seem affected.

"You okay?" he asked.

"Mhm," I said, rubbing the back of my hand across my forehead. "I-I think I'm going to go to bed now."

He nodded, watching me suspiciously as I walked from the room. I hit the stairs quickly, my movements feeling sluggish as my eyes began to droop. I made it to the top of the stairs before my knees gave out and I dropped to the ground. If he found me there, he'd know something was wrong. I knew that. I knew I was setting myself up for trouble, yet I couldn't move. I couldn't make my muscles do what I needed them to, couldn't make my mind care.

As I faded off into a deep slumber, I remember hearing the front door slam. Was someone coming or going? I had no idea. I had no idea about anything anymore.

THE NEXT THING I REMEMBER, the front doorbell was ringing. I opened my eyes slowly, surprised to see so much light around me. It was morning and I was still alive, though I didn't know how or why.

The doorbell rang again, and I edged myself down the stairs, groaning with each bump. I tried to piece together my memories of the night, wondering what day or time it was. When I reached the living room, I glanced at the clock. It was almost noon. Mark's jacket and keys were missing from their places.

I pulled open the door, still utterly confused and trying to force my sleep-coated mind to clear. The police officers stood in front of me, and I lunged for them, everything coming back to me all at once. I was screaming something about my husband and how he was trying to kill me. I don't think the words made any sense as they mixed with tears and snot. I may have thrown up, too. I can't even remember, truth be told.

What I do remember, though, is one of the officers grabbing my arms. His voice was loud and deep, like the man from the old Allstate commercials. He placed his face in front of mine and managed to cut through all the fog of my brain as he spoke.

"You're safe, Mrs. Oliver. You're safe. Your husband can't hurt you."

"You don't know that," I argued, struggling against his grip as I tried to look behind me, sure Mark would be coming out from wherever he was soon. "He has a gun. He's going to kill me!"

"Ma'am, your husband can't kill anyone," he said firmly. "Do you hear me? Mark's dead. Your husband is dead."

I collapsed then, my knees buckling so quickly I slammed onto the porch. "W-what?"

"I'm so sorry," he said, kneeling down in front of me. "Your husband was in a car accident early this morning. He was driving and hit a divider. The car flipped. He…he died on impact."

"Mark is…"

"That's right," he told me. "He's dead."

CHAPTER TWENTY-NINE

HER

PRESENT DAY

"If what you're telling me is true, Mrs. Oliver—"

"Hannah, please," I correct him, unsure why he's choosing to call me Mrs. Oliver now. "I'll be changing my name soon enough."

"Hannah," my lawyer says, dipping his head down with respect. "If what you're telling me is true, you didn't *kill* your husband. Not enough to convict you of murder anyway. It was manslaughter at best, and with your testimony—"

"I don't want to testify," I say. "I deserve to go to prison."

"Why do you say that?" he asks, laying down his pen. "You were trying to protect yourself. You believed your husband was going to kill you."

"I jumped to conclusions. My husband was a violent man, an angry man, but I killed him. His actions don't justify mine."

"That's not your job to decide. The jury will—"

"I don't want a jury."

"We may not even need a jury. If we can explain what's happened, they may let you plea down anyway."

"All due respect, counselor, I want to take the plea deal the prosecutor has already offered. I want to serve my time and move on with my life."

His gray brows furrow. "Now, your parents didn't hire me so I could get you a basic plea deal like the one they're offering. Any cut-rate legal defender could do that."

"Then perhaps I need to get one of those." I fold my hands on the table in front of me.

"Why are you so dead set on going to jail?" he asks. "I don't understand."

"Because I made a mistake. I'm no better than Mark."

"Your husband raped McKenna Logan, he beat you nearly to death—"

"And I murdered him."

"You didn't hold a gun to his head, Hannah."

"I may as well have. He told me he wasn't going to kill me. I could've waited and left once things had calmed down."

"You didn't know that!"

"I didn't know half of what I thought I did, and now we both know that."

He leans away from me in his chair, one arm thrown over the back. "So what do you want me to do?"

"I want you to do your job, Mr. Cavendish, and at the moment that job is to do what I've asked you to do. So, bring me the papers and let me sign whatever deal they've offered, and let's get this over with, shall we?"

He sighs at me, and I can see the years of age his troublesome clients have added to his face. "You're making a mistake."

I wrinkle my nose at him, picking at a piece of skin near my nail. "I've done that before."

"You couldn't have known!"

"I should have. I should have known," I say, feeling my eyes brim with fresh tears. "There's one last thing I haven't told you, and…it changes everything."

CHAPTER THIRTY

HER

THE DAY OF MARK'S DEATH

I lied before when I told you the only place I went the morning I left the house was to the grocery store where I ran into McKenna. I did a few things before that. I was suspicious. I'd let it go, but I kept thinking back to that letter I'd found on Mark's computer. The one I'd dismissed as being for a client. With all the new things I was finding out about him, about his past and the secrets it held, and then all the new allegations, it felt like my duty to get to know the man I'd married before he became the man I'd married.

I needed to know the truth about everything.

My first stop was to head to the bar where Mark and I first met. I knew from the day of his first accident that he was still a regular customer. I wasn't sure exactly what I hoped to find there, but it seemed like if anyone knew my husband better than I did, it would be his old bar family.

Vic was wiping down the counter when I walked in.

She was the last person I was hoping to talk to, honestly. I was hoping to see the waiter from before.

"Can I help you?" Vic asked. "We aren't open yet." I could tell by her determined expression she was trying to figure out where she knew me from.

"Oh, I know. Sorry," I rushed toward the counter so I wasn't having to yell across the room. "I, um, I'm Hannah. Ol—"

"Oliver," she finished for me. "I knew you looked familiar."

"Yes, well—"

"How's Mark? He here with you?" She looked over my shoulder with wide, hopeful eyes.

"No, he's not, it's just me. Actually, I was hoping to ask someone a few questions about him."

She picked up a glass, shining it with the same rag she'd just used on the counter. "Ask away."

"I'm hoping this can stay between us. I mean, I know you're friends…"

"I hardly know Mark, except for when he comes in here for drinks. Truth be told, some of the guys love him, but he's never been a very good tipper. That kind of makes him just a customer, you know? No offense. I know he's your husband." She shrugged. "He's hot. I get it. But still…kind of a jerk."

I smirked. "No offense taken. So, you didn't know him from college?"

"No, just here. Why?"

I shook my head. "I was hoping to find someone who knew him from college. For a…birthday surprise."

She wiggled her eyebrows. "Oooh, a threesome?"

173

My eyes grew wide, and I shook my head sharply. "No!"

She laughed and offered me a wink. "Hey, I didn't go to college, but even I can tell you *that* would be the best birthday gift you could give him. Anyway, just a sec." She disappeared behind the bar, leaving me to stare at the words and names carved into its wood. I ran my fingers along a set of initials, thinking of all the possibilities that started here.

When Vic came back, she was holding a business card. "Here. You should contact Arizona Ferris. She manages the bank on the corner of Fifth and Elm. She's come in here a few times to meet with Mark. They seem like just friends, but I remember Mark always introduced her as an old college buddy. Maybe she can help you with what-ever it is you're looking for."

I stared at the business card, wondering why I'd never heard of Arizona Ferris. "Thank you," I told her, glancing up at her. "This helps a ton. Do you...I mean, should I take a photo of it?"

"Keep it," she said with a wave of her hand. "She leaves stacks of them every time she's in. Our patrons aren't exactly the money market crowd, anyway."

"Thank you, Vic," I said again. "And if you could please just remember to keep this—"

She held up two fingers. "Just between us. You have my word."

With that, I dashed out of the bar and back out onto the crowded street. I looked at the address on the business card, searching for a street sign that matched. Finally, I saw a blue logo on a building that matched the one on the card in my hand. I crossed the street and headed a block up until I reached my destination.

The bank was small; they had just a limited amount of space on the first floor. The layout was different than I expected. It had been years since I'd actually had to go inside a bank, though. I guess the banking industry had changed a bit. The row of tellers I was used to was down to just two smiling faces, and there was an ATM in the middle of the lobby.

"Hello there," one teller said, offering up a smile. "I can help you over here. What can I do for you?" She patted the window in front of her, and I approached her station.

"I'm looking for your manager…Arizona?" I held up the business card.

"Of course," she said. "If you'd like to have a seat, I'll let her know you're waiting. Is she expecting you?"

I shook my head.

"No worries," she said, picking up the phone. "Just have a seat. Help yourself to a bottle of water or a cup of coffee."

No sooner had I sat down, than a door to an office on my right opened and out glided a redheaded woman, her heels clicking loudly on the floor.

"Hi!" she said, her voice too cheery. "I'm Arizona." I stood as she stretched her arm out to shake my hand. "How can I help you?"

"My name's Hannah Oliver, I think you know my husband, Mark."

I tried to see if her eyes grew dark or fearful, but to my relief, they didn't. "I do, yes. Is everything okay?"

"Could we…um, go in your office? It's kind of private."

"Of course," she said, stepping back and holding out her arm for me to lead the way. She was trying to decide why I was there, but I didn't sense any true worry. Perhaps she and Mark truly had been *just* friends after all. I would expect an old girlfriend to hold more resentment than she was exhibiting.

Once we were in her office, she shut the door and took a seat across from me. "Now, then, Mrs. Oliver, what can I do for you?" She was pretty in a traditional way, porcelain skin and dark brown eyes that stood out against her bright red hair.

"Just, just Hannah, please. I, um, I'm trying to find out some information about my husband's past. I checked the bar where he used to work, and they said you guys go there together sometimes."

"We do," she said, then shrugged. "Only once or twice, though; it's certainly not a regular thing. I've been trying to get his firm's accounts since he started there. I can assure you we're just friends, if that's what this is about." She wagged her fingers in the air, showing off a large diamond ring set before she turned a picture on her desk around so I could see her family. A husband and two children—they were a picture-perfect crew.

"They're gorgeous," I told her.

"Thank you," she said, smiling humbly. "So, what did you need to know about Mark?" She crossed her hands in front of her on the desk, getting down to business.

"You went to college with him, right?"

"I did." She blinked, her face showing no emotion.

"So, you probably know a little about his struggles with alcohol?"

I watched her shoulders tense a bit, and she glanced down. "Mark hadn't mentioned it, no, but I suspected."

"Suspected?"

She glanced down at her fingers, twisting one around the other as she explained. "He didn't drink when we were at the bar together. Only sodas. That…wasn't like Mark."

"I'm…worried about him, Arizona. He told me recently that alcohol has made him do some very bad things. Do you have any idea what that could mean?"

She shook her head, twisting her lips. "I don't really know. You didn't ask him?"

"I did, but he got very closed off. He thinks I won't look at him the same if I know what he was like before, but I need to know. He's drinking again, and it's starting to get bad. I don't want it to get any worse, and if me knowing how bad he's been can prevent that somehow, I need to know."

"I'm sorry," she said, wringing her fingers together in front of her. "I don't think I'll be much help. The Mark that I knew in college was fun. He was a partier, sure, but his drinking only made him more social. Was it a buffer or a way of distracting himself from something? Probably, but we were kids. We didn't ask any questions like we should have. Last I talked to Mark, he was sober and doing well for himself. I thought he'd worked through all of his issues."

"So did I," I said. "It's just been recently that he's back to drinking, and I want to help him so badly, but I don't know how." I paused. "Well, okay. Thank you for your time." I started to stand, but her hand jerked out to stop me.

"Mark would kill me if I told you this," she said, not meeting my eyes.

"What is it?" I sank back down, leaning forward on her desk.

"I don't know if it's true, but if you're digging, well, back when we were in school, there were these...rumors."

"What sort of rumors?"

"Morgan Smith, have you heard her name?"

I shook my head. "Not that I can recall."

"She went to school with us, was friends with our group for a while. But one day, she just didn't come to class. And the next day, we heard she'd dropped out." She chewed on her fingernail nervously, thinking. "Rumor had it that Mark had something to do with it. He denied it, of course, and even after we reconnected years later, I couldn't get the truth out of either of them. But Morgan won't have anything to do with Mark even to this day. We used to all be inseparable."

I stared at her, letting what she was telling me sink in. "Okay," I said. "So, do you know how to contact her?"

"She lives in Senoia. It's a half hours' drive. I can give you her cell, but if Mark finds out about this, you didn't hear it from me."

"Of course." She grabbed a sticky note and her phone, copying down a number onto the pink paper and handing it over.

"Hannah," she said, gripping the paper firmly between her fingers before letting it slide into mine. "If any of it's true, would you please be careful, with whatever you find out about him? He had a rough beginning, I think. Shit dad, absent mother, pretty awkward kid." She offered a sad smile out of the side of her mouth. "But he's not a bad guy, I don't think. He just doesn't know how healthy humans are supposed to be. He's helped me through a lot. Just…I guess what I'm saying is, take care of him, will you?"

I nodded. "Of course I will." I looked down at the note, feeling one step closer to everything I'd need to do just that. "Thank you, Arizona. For everything."

"I hope you find what you're looking for. I hope you can help him." She stood as I made my way out the door.

"Me, too," I whispered, already dialing the number in my hand.

———

AN HOUR LATER, I was meeting Morgan at a local coffee shop in downtown Senoia. The small town was buzzing with people, and I'd heard they were filming a television show just down the road, which accounted for even heavier traffic. I'd had trouble finding a spot to park, in fact.

Morgan worked at the coffee shop, and she'd asked that I meet her there during her break. I had no idea what to expect. There were dozens of Morgan Smiths on Facebook, so though I'd tried to look her up, I had no idea what she looked like and couldn't truly keep an eye out for her.

When a woman with long, curly brown hair approached my table, I took in the sight of her blue eyes and small, puckered lips. "Morgan?" I stood. She nodded and took my hand as I reached out. "I'm Hannah."

"I know," she said.

"You do?"

"I looked you up when I found out he'd gotten married. You look the same as in your pictures."

It seemed like an odd thing to say. Why was she keeping tabs on Mark? How did she know we'd gotten married? "Oh," I said finally, because something needed to fill the silence.

"So, what can I do for you?" She sat down across from me.

"I was hoping you could tell me more about who Mark was before I met him. He seems to be hiding something from his past from me and, well, I spoke to someone who went to school with you all, and she said maybe I could talk to you."

She crossed her arms over her chest and leaned back in her chair with a tight jaw. "Arizona needs to learn to keep her nose out of it."

"I didn't—"

"I know it was Arizona," she said. "She texted to tell me to talk to you."

"Oh, okay. Yeah. So, will you? Talk to me, I mean."

"What is it you want to know?"

"Well, Mark's drinking can get out of control. He was sober for a while, when we met, but he's drinking again, and I can't figure out how to help him. When we talk about it, he just shuts down, but I get the feeling something in his past really haunts him. I'm not sure what you know about it or if you know anything—"

"Oh, I know plenty," she said with a dry laugh. "I know all about how poor, tortured Mark Oliver had such a bad childhood that he gets to grow up and make life miserable for the rest of us. Listen, if I were you, I'd get as far away from him as possible and never look back. Disappear altogether if that's what it takes to be free of him. Don't let him hurt you, Hannah. He's ruined enough lives."

I swallowed. "You mean yours?"

"Mine," she said with a nod, "but plenty of others, too."

"What did he do?"

"Are you going to leave him if I tell you?"

"I-I don't know," I said honestly. "I want to get him help. I don't want to give up on him when he's so obviously sick."

"He's beyond help, Hannah. If you think you can help him, what I'm going to tell you will only make your job harder. You came to the wrong place if you want to be told there's hope for your husband."

"He must've really hurt you," I said, my head tilted to the side. "Arizona said you dropped out of school, and she thought it might have something to do with him."

"It had everything to do with him," she said in a huff.

"Can you tell me what happened?"

"The last time I told someone, it hurt that person. Someone else I cared about very much. I can't keep letting Mark hurt people."

"Don't you think I deserve to know?" I asked.

She narrowed her eyes into a scowl at me. "You're just like him, aren't you? Always thinking about what *you* deserve and what the world owes you? Well, I don't owe you the truth, Hannah, I don't. If you want to know what happened between us, you need to ask Mark."

"He won't tell me!" I said, gripping the edge of the table. "And nothing gets solved if I don't know."

"Nothing gets solved if you do know, either. You just feel worse."

"I have money," I said, gesturing toward my purse. "Is that what you want? If I pay you, will you tell me?"

Her expression turned icy in an instant, and I knew I'd said the wrong thing. "You really are just like him. I don't need your money. Either of yours. I told Mark that months ago. I may not live in a townhouse in Atlanta, but I can take care of myself."

"Mark offered you money?" I asked, glaring at her. "What are you talking about? How do you know where we live?"

"Forget it," she said. "I'm sorry you wasted your trip. I can't help you."

She moved to stand, and I reached for her hand out of instinct. "Please," I begged. "Please tell me what's going on. If I'm in danger, if my husband is in danger…I want to know. Woman to woman, I'm asking you."

She shook her head. "What good will it do? You've already made up your mind about him. You think he's fixable, but I know he's not."

"I'm here, aren't I?" I asked. "I want to know the truth, and obviously I can't trust him to give it to me. I haven't made up my mind about him because I apparently don't know the man I married very well at all."

"You don't," she agreed. "The man you married is one version of Mark Oliver. When he's good he's…very, *very* good. But when Mark's bad, he's pure evil." The way her eyes went blank as she spoke of him sent chills down my spine.

"What did he do to you, Morgan?"

Her pale hands shook as she picked at the skin around her nails. "We were just kids, you know? I trusted him. He was my *friend.* I never in a million years thought he could —" She stifled a sob, her hands clutching her stomach. I waited patiently for her to go on, though I had a feeling I already knew where it was going. "We were at a party together, all of us. I'll never know why it was me he chose, instead of Arizona or Clarissa or Jeanie. Was I just the weakest one? He knew I couldn't fight back, I guess. Arizona's parents were powerful and Clarissa was well liked. I was quiet. Shy. He saw that, you know? He picked me from the very beginning. I would've never been friends with that group if Mark hadn't initiated it. But he did, and he waited months before he…" She stopped, pressing her hands into her stomach as she took deliberate breaths. "I was weak then, but I'm not now. I let him hurt me because I didn't know how to fight back. I dropped out of school, never told a soul what happened. They wouldn't believe me anyway, he said. We were friends, we'd flirted. I even had a crush on him at one point, and everyone knew it. He'd tell them that I asked for it. Things weren't like they are now, you know? It wasn't even that long ago, but I was a nobody and he was popular and handsome. He could have had anyone he wanted, so why would he have to f-f-force m-m—" She was shaking with sobs, and I stood, moving to the chair next to her so I could hold her through her tears. She shoved me back, wiping her eyes. "I'm fine," she said quickly.

"You don't have to be fine. I'm so sorry, Morgan. I'm so sorry."

"You believe me?" she asked.

I nodded and watched more tears well in her eyes. "I believe you."

"Then you need to leave him, or it'll be you next. He's smart, Hannah. He finds your weaknesses and exposes them." I'd already experienced that with the way he manipulated my need for a family. Like a toy he dangled above my head when he needed something.

"But why did he offer you money? Were you threatening to come forward with your story?"

"Of course not," she said. "I've moved on from what happened." She sniffled, grabbing a tissue from the middle of our table and dabbing her eyes. "No, I contacted Mark because—" She paused, her eyes dancing around the busy street before they landed back on me. "After I left school, I found out I was pregnant. I have a son."

I gasped, the weight of what she was saying slamming into my chest and stealing my breath. "He's Mark's?"

"He's mine," she said. "He never belonged to Mark. He was...*is* a good boy. Troubled, but good. Boys without their fathers, they, well, they get into trouble now and again. The school counselors always told me it was normal. He'd grow out of it. But he got to an age where he started having questions about his father, and I made up a story about a boy I loved in college who'd died. I made up a father who loved him. Who loved me. I made a fairytale out of my nightmare. When Damon turned eighteen, he did some kind of ancestry kit and it connected him to Mark. I tried to tell him there'd been a mistake, but he tracked him down. It wasn't hard to find him on the internet, and without telling me, he traveled to his work and found him." She paused. "Did you know?"

I shook my head, unable to form words. How was any of this possible? How had I not known?

"Figures he wouldn't tell you. Mark always cared about his perfect image much more than the truth. Which is exactly why, when Damon found Mark, Mark told him he'd never known about him. He didn't want to look like the monster that he was. That's when he sent me some email about sending me money if I promised not to contact him again. But we didn't want his money. I wanted nothing to do with him, but I couldn't enforce that on Damon, as much as I tried."

My mind flashed back to the email I'd found on his computer, the one I couldn't stop thinking about. Another lie. Another secret. More of his past coming back to haunt us. The cloud of darkness that seemed to follow my husband kept growing.

"I never wanted his money, but I owed my son the truth. When I told him, when I told him how he'd come to be, Damon was distraught. He claimed I was lying. Said that I just didn't want him to know his father. Said that I was the reason Mark wasn't in his life. That was…over a year ago, and I can count on one hand the number of times I've seen my son since."

"What happened to him?"

"He got lost," she said simply. "In every sense of the word. He's an addict, like his father, but it goes much deeper than alcohol. He's delusional and addicted to the idea of what could've been. Addicted to a fantasy life I can't give him. He changed his name, calls himself 'Mark' now. He lives on the streets most days. I've had him committed. I've tried to get him help, but he doesn't want it. Mark ruined my life, and then I let him ruin my son's, and there was nothing I could do about it."

"What about rehab? Surely there's something the doctors can do," I said. "I can help pay for it. With my money, not Mark's. It doesn't have to have anything to do with him. He doesn't have to know."

She smiled at me, the first genuine smile I'd seen. "That's kind of you, but even if I could find Damon, he wouldn't stay in psychiatric care for long. I took out a second mortgage on my house to pay for it before, and he checked himself out within a week. His doctors say until he wants to get better, he won't, and I've just got to accept that."

"That's not fair," I said, reaching for her hand. To my surprise, she let me hold it, just for a second, before pulling it away. She grabbed her phone from her pocket and spun it around to me so I could see the screen. A teenage boy with dark hair and bright blue eyes smiled up at me, one wiry arm wrapped around a happy Morgan. I lifted the phone so I could get a better look. If I'd wanted to deny her story before, there was no way I could've then.

"That's my boy, my Damon." She cleared her throat. "Before."

As I stared at the photo, it was as if a younger Mark was staring back at me, everything from the same dimple in his left cheek to the way he held his head, always to one side.

"He's beautiful," I told her.

"He's a good boy. He's just…hurt, right now."

"We're going to make this okay, Morgan. I'm going to get your son the help he needs. I promise you that." And as I stared into her eyes, so full of pain and heartache, I meant it more than I'd ever meant anything in my life.

CHAPTER THIRTY-ONE

HIM

THEN

W hen I met my dad for the first time, he had no idea who I was, or that I even existed. I didn't understand it at first, but I do now. I know that it was my mom's fault. I know that she was selfish and chose to keep me to herself. I understand that women are selfish manipulators and we can't trust them.

She named me Damon, but I've always hated it. Hated the way she called me 'Dame' for short. Like a girl.

When I met my dad, I saw power. I saw the way he wore a suit that Mom could've never afforded. I saw the way the people in his office looked up to him. Respected him. I've never had that before.

But when I was with him, when I was *Mark*, I did. People treated me differently. No longer was I the son of a waitress. Now, now I am the son of a lawyer.

See that? Your ears perked up when you heard it, didn't they? Because they're two different people. Who I was and who I am. Damon and Mark. My dad said he'd always hoped to have a son who could be his namesake, like he was his grandfather's. He said it was the ultimate honor.

So, when I told him I'd like to take his name, I was giving him a gift. A gift like the one he gave me when he told me the truth about how I came into the world. About how much he loved my mom and how she disappeared and took me away from him without telling him she was pregnant. My dad gave me the truth, and that's a gift that's incredibly rare.

For months now, I've been visiting with my dad during the week. We meet at his office, and he takes me to lunch. Pays for it and everything. A few times, he's even taken me to a bar across town. The drinks there are like twenty dollars, but he can afford it. It's crazy the way he lives. Oh, and his car? It's worth more than our entire house.

He wanted to bring me home to live with him, to give me a life of luxury like the one he lived, but there was one problem.

Hannah.

I crack my knuckles just thinking of her. I hate her. How could a smart guy like my dad have chosen someone so horrible?

He asked her if I could live there, but she said no. If you want my opinion, he shouldn't have had to ask. It's his money that pays for everything. He told me she doesn't even work. But nope. She didn't want me there. I wasn't her child, and she wanted nothing to do with me.

He told me how she wants children of her own—their

own. A child to replace me. I didn't want that to happen. I couldn't let it. I wanted her gone, I didn't want more of a reason for him to be attached to her more than me.

For a while, he let me sleep in his office overnight. He'd come in early and get me to leave before the rest of his team showed up. But then he got fired because one of the sluts in the office wanted to fuck him and he said no.

Can you believe it? He said no and they still fired him!

Bunch of assholes.

He was going to be just fine, though. Dad was a fighter. He would come out on top, he promised. He just needed time to figure everything out, and I wanted to help him.

I'd never hurt anyone before, not unless you count arm wrestling my best friend Dylan in school, but I knew what needed to be done in order for my dad to be happy again, and that's all I wanted.

I followed the girl home from work, the one who told all the lies about him, after he told me what happened. Once I'd found her house, I watched her, learned her routine. I'd seen it on *Criminal Minds*, how to stalk. I was excellent at it. I'd always been good at keeping quiet. When I was young, Mom would bring me to work with her when she couldn't afford a sitter, and she'd tell me to keep quiet in the office. Most days, no one even knew I was there.

I took my time coming up with a plan of what to do with the girl. That's how killers always get caught, they aren't patient. But I was. I waited a week, made sure I had everything planned out, and then I knew it was time. I made my move.

I remember the way my hand felt, pulsing with power as it connected with the wood of her door.

I remember her eyes, wide with fear when she saw me. "Do I know you?" she asked. She'd met me three times, and she didn't recognize me, *stupid bitch.* She was just like all the other women. I couldn't offer her anything, so she forgot me.

"I'm here for Mark," I said, pulling the gun from my jacket pocket. It was heavier than I'd expected. I'd never actually shot it, but the guy I bought it from showed me how it worked. It was a lot of money, and I don't have a lot. Not yet. I had to trade one of Mark's watches for it, but I'd planned to put it back before he even noticed. Besides, this was more important.

"Mark?" she asked, her head cocked to the side, eyes crossing as they stared at the barrel. "What are you talking abou—"

I didn't let her finish. I squeezed the trigger, shutting her up once and for all. The shot shook my arm and it hit her cheek, but she fell to the ground and didn't move. I remember her scream, the way it stopped short when the bullet connected. I stood above her, watching the blood pour out of her face and pool beneath her.

I'd done it.

I'd killed her.

With her gone, Dad's job could be saved.

Then everything would be okay.

Well, once I got rid of Hannah.

CHAPTER THIRTY-TWO

HIM

I went to Dad's house that night to tell him what I'd done, to tell him I'd saved him. I could hear them yelling inside. I could hear Hannah screaming at him. Him defending himself. Why did he love her so much? I still don't understand it. She was cruel to him.

I guess she'd found out about the girl from work, but she didn't know he was innocent. I sat on their porch for a long time, listening to them fighting. It was all I could do not to go inside and help him, but he'd made me swear not to let Hannah ever see me. He told me she'd lose it if she did.

I waited and waited, hoping she'd go to bed. Finally, when it got quiet, I knocked on the door. I could see Dad moving around in the living room. He lifted his head, but instead of a smile on his face, he frowned at me.

He was angry that I'd showed up. I told him what I did. I told him that the girl was dead, that I could take care of Hannah if I needed to. I was inside of his house for the first time, and it just felt right, you know? I knew I was supposed to be there all along.

It was like the start of our lives together. Father and son forever.

I could see Hannah's body at the top of the stairs. She was drunk. Passed out like a whore. Dad said she'd always been a drinker. I knew then what I needed to do. What I had to do to fix everything. All it would take was one shot. One shot and she'd be out of our hair forever. It was that easy. I was going to take care of it all. I showed him the gun and told him my plan.

But he wouldn't let me do it. He told me we had to leave. He told me the police were on their way for me and he wanted to protect me. There was no time for finishing off loose ends right then. We grabbed the keys and headed out the door. He didn't even pack anything because I was all that was important to him left in the world. We were going to run away together.

But when we got going, he was swerving all over. He couldn't keep his eyes open. I don't remember crossing the lanes, but I remember the way the headlights looked on the concrete wall that we hit.

I tried to grab the wheel, but his head fell onto me. He was so heavy for being so thin. Muscle, I guess. The next thing I knew, we were upside down and there was glass everywhere. I'd banged my head, but I could still see. I yelled for Dad, but he didn't answer.

I yelled and I yelled and I yelled, but he wouldn't answer.

That's when I realized he was dead. And I was alone again.

Story of my life.

CHAPTER THIRTY-THREE

HIM

PRESENT DAY

My idiot lawyer is droning on about charges and prison again, but I mostly tune him out. I don't care about me. I don't care what happens. What I care about is Hannah, and making sure she goes to jail for the rest of her life. Or dies. Either way, I guess. Maybe both. Maybe we'll both go to prison, and then, if I see her in there, I'll kill her. "Damon, I hope you realize, the charges against you are serious—"

"Mark, dammit, *Mark*! How many times do I have to tell you I don't go by my first name?"

"Be that as it may, your legal name *is* Damon. You are not your father. You are not Mark. To go on pretending otherwise would be a disservice to you."

"Fuck you," I tell him, kicking the table in front of me. It doesn't move because it's bolted to the floor, but he gets the point. If I had my gun, he'd be next.

His fat forehead wrinkles, and he clicks his pen closed.

"I have someone here who'd like to see you." He stands and waddles toward the door, opening it slowly. When he steps back, I see my mom.

I still have mixed feelings about her. On one hand I love her, but on the other, she's lied to me my whole life, and now my time with my dad is cut even shorter. Still, I lean in for the hug she offers.

There are tears in her eyes, and I feel pretty bad about that.

"I'm okay, Mom," I tell her, because I am.

She nods, her lips moving like she wants to say something, but she doesn't. "I want you to listen to Mr. Cavendish," she said. "We've got some doctors who want to help you. He thinks he can get it so they can lessen your sentence if you will agree to get help."

I flick a booger across the room and bite the inside of my lip until it bleeds. "What if I don't want help?"

"D-Damon, you need help. You know that, right, sweetie? You know that what you did was wrong, don't you?" She is begging, which Dad says they do when they're desperate. She's desperate for me to say yes, but I don't. What I did was take care of someone I love; that can't be wrong.

"I don't think it was wrong."

"You...you killed someone." She glances at my lawyer, and I see him give her a strange look.

"People die all the time." It's a fact, and I don't know why I can't say that it is. When I was growing up, Mom always corrected me when I told her these facts. She told me I should feel sad about death when my grandfather died, but I didn't. I'm not really sure what *sad* means. If it means I wanted to play marbles with him again and I couldn't, then, sure, I guess I was sad.

"So?" I roll my eyes at her frown. People make such a big deal out of that stupid emotion: sadness. I don't get it. It's honestly not that bad. Anger, now there's an emotion. Nothing more powerful in the world.

"Damon, this is serious," she says, and her voice is louder, which means she's upset. "You have to do what they tell you. Do you hear me? You have to!"

"I can do whatever I want," I tell her, kicking my feet up on the table. "And I've told you to *call me Mark*." I growl at her, so sick of having to repeat myself.

"Don't you want to get out of here?" she asks me, shaking her head as she speaks.

"If you let me out, I'll kill her," I tell her.

"Damon, don't—"

"My name is Mark!" I yell, leaning up in her face. I hope my breath stinks. If she wasn't my mother, I'd want her dead, too. *Anger. Anger. Anger. Anger.*

"Mark," she corrects with a shaking voice. She takes a step back, a sign of submission. I've won. "Don't say that, sweetheart."

"It's the truth, Mom." I smile at her the way she hates, so my teeth look like fangs. "And if you've taught me anything…it's that the truth, even when it's bad, even when it's ugly, is always worth telling."

CHAPTER THIRTY-FOUR

PRESENT DAY

My lawyer comes back into the room, and I push my feet against the floor to sit up straighter.

"If you'll agree to a plea deal, the State will do five years plus a years' probation."

"Done," I say, "where do I sign?"

He sits down in front of me, shaking his head. "You don't have to do this, Hannah. I'm telling you, I think I can get you out of here with no prison time at all. What you did was an accident. It wasn't premeditated. The State knows it. You know it. I know it. What's the problem?"

"The problem is that, with what *Damon-Mark-whatever he calls himself* has told us, I could've been dead. My husband's last act on this earth was to spare my life, and he died because of it."

"Because he chose to drive drunk."

"But he wrecked because of the massive amounts of sleeping pills in his system. We all know that, too."

"You weren't responsible—"

"I damn well was," I cry out. "And I have to live with that. My husband was a rapist. He was violent. He was a liar. But he wasn't a killer. He chose to save my life, and I ended his, and now I've seen what his victims do to their children..." I break off, letting out a sob I'd sworn to myself I wouldn't.

"Their children?" he asks, his head tilting to the side as he tries to understand. "Damon?"

I nod. "Mark ruined him. The damage he did to Morgan ruined him."

"Hannah, I'm no doctor, but I can tell you that what Damon's got going on goes much deeper than just daddy issues, okay? He needs help. His mother didn't see that, but it's not her fault. It's not anyone's fault. It just needs to be fixed."

"And what if it can't? What if *she* can't do it? What if it's done?"

"What if she can't do what?"

"What if she can't fix him? What if she can't fix a child like that?"

"What are you even talking about? Damon won't be allowed to come around you, if that's what you're afraid of. Even if he gets off, which, between you and I, he doesn't seem interested in doing, he will still be in a psychiatric hospital for a long time."

"But I knew about him. I knew he existed, and instead of telling Mark I knew, I let him keep his secret. Now McKenna is dead because of it. I could've stopped this. I could've stopped all of this." I place my face in my palms and shake with sobs.

He taps the table with his forefinger and leans in close. "McKenna is dead because a very sick boy killed her, not because of you. You couldn't have prevented that, and punishing yourself isn't going to help anyone."

"I'm not punishing myself, I'm protecting my child!" I shout, looking up at him as my hand moves instinctively toward my stomach.

"Your..." He stops talking, staring at me in shock. "Are you pregnant?"

"I haven't taken a test, but I'm late. And this child belongs to Mark. He has every bit of Mark's DNA that Damon has. What if Mark's the problem? What if he's passed the same problems down to this baby? What if it's in Mark's DNA? What if a woman who's been raped by Mark can't raise a normal child? Because I think I have been. I wasn't sure before, but I think so now. What if my child—" I am nearing hysterics when he cuts me off.

"Let me stop you," he says, reaching for my hand. "What you're doing is panicking, and I understand why, but worrying about all these things without any answers won't help you. What are you hoping for? That you'll go to prison and it'll ease the pain of having your child taken away from you?"

I nod. That's exactly what I'm hoping, thank you very much. "I forced him to try for a child."

"You wanted to be a mother."

"What if my child is a monster?" I ask, my voice coming out as a high-pitched whimper.

He sighs, and I don't at all like the all-knowing way he is staring at me. "That's not really what you're asking, is it?"

I feel my chin quivering as my tears begin to spill over. "What if *I'm* the monster? How could I have been married to someone like Mark and not have known who or what he was? How could I not have seen the signs?"

"Are you a trained psychologist?"

"Of course not."

"No one else would be expected to see those signs."

"How many nights did I fall asleep holding the hands that had ripped the clothes off some helpless girl just hours before? If I couldn't see that, how will I see the signs when my child needs my help?"

"You aren't responsible for anything your husband did, do you hear me? There are monsters in this story, Hannah, don't get me wrong. Plenty of them, going back many generations. But you are not one of them. What happened here happened *to* you, not because of you. And the way I see it, you have two options. One, you can give up. Go to prison. Let your child be raised by someone else while you sit around like a wounded dog and wait for your life to pass you by. Or two, you can fight back. Take your life back. You can say the ripple effect of Mark's evil ends here." He shoved his forefinger down on the tabletop. "With you. You can tell the judge your story, go home, and have your baby. You can raise it with love and happiness and joy. You can raise it to not know the bitterness that its father would've introduced it to. You spared this baby a lifetime filled with all of that. You did it, Hannah. You *protected* your child. You can love this baby, and you can learn to love yourself again, too. You can do all that in spite of Mark, not because of him or what he's done. His touch on your life ends the second you decide it does, and not a moment before."

I sniffle, running a finger under my nose. "I think *you* missed your calling as a trained psychologist."

He smiles at me, and his expression is so warm I have to smile, too. "I have kids. Giving advice comes with the territory. Something you'll learn soon enough." He shifts in his chair. "I can't make the decision for you, Hannah. But if you let this happen, if you sign this paper in my hands, he wins. You can glorify what he did in his last hour, saving your life, but the fact is that he lived his life as a monster. He monopolized the bad things that happened to him and used them as an excuse to mistreat and control those around him. Don't let him control you anymore. Don't let him win."

"What if I can't do this? What if I don't have any good-ness left in me after what I've been through?"

"You do—"

"You don't know that."

He nods and reaches for my hand, his touch calming down the panic that was beginning to set in again. "I do. I do know that. I know that because you asked your parents to pay for Damon's lawyer. I know that because you want to see him get the help he needs despite the fact that he's dead set on killing you. I know that because you want to protect this child, even if it costs you what you've wanted your whole life. *You are good*, Hannah. Mark didn't take that from you."

I nod, chewing my lip as I think. I follow a procedure that Doctor Fremont taught us in therapy. I close my eyes, and I think of all the bad that Mark has done. All the lies and the manipulation. Then, I think of all the good in my life: my parents, my old job, Luis, this baby—the size of a mustard seed—growing inside my belly. As terrified as I am, Mr. Cavendish is right. I need to keep moving. Keep going, if not for my own sake, for the sake of my child, whose mere existence offers me a fresh start wherever I end up.

"Okay," I say finally, opening my eyes.

"Okay?" he asks, a smile growing on his wrinkled face. "Atta girl. Now, let me go back and talk to the prosecutor. I'll be in touch, okay?"

I nod, already allowing hope to fill me. It's been a long time since I've felt it. Before he reaches the door to call the bailiff back to me, he turns to meet my eyes. "Everything's going to be okay now. You know that, right?"

I smile with a grin that shows all my teeth and run a hand across the baby that will save my life, just as I saved his. "Yes."

DON'T MISS THE NEXT
PSYCHOLOGICAL THRILLER FROM
KIERSTEN MODGLIN!

What she doesn't know about her new family could
kill her...

Read *The Mother-in-Law* today:
https://amzn.to/2vnfMic

DON'T MISS THE NEXT KIERSTEN MODGLIN RELEASE!

Thank you so much for reading this story. I'd love to invite you to sign up for my mailing list and text alerts so we can be sure you don't miss my next release.

Sign up for my mailing list here:
http://eepurl.com/dhiRRv
Sign up for my text alerts here:
www.kierstenmodglinauthor.com/textalerts.html

ENJOYED I SAID YES?

If you enjoyed this story, please consider leaving me a quick review. It doesn't have to be long—just a few words will do. Who knows? Your review might be the thing that encourages a future reader to take a chance on my work!

To leave a review, please visit:

https://amzn.to/30XX1gv

Check out *I Said Yes* on Goodreads:

http://bit.ly/36tfpQE

ACKNOWLEDGMENTS

When I decided to chase this amazing dream, there were so many people who said *yes,* I could do it. Now that I've been in this amazing book-world for quite some time, there are so many people who say *yes* everyday by purchasing my books, leaving me reviews, and sharing my name. To them, I owe all the thanks.

To *my husband, Michael, and my daughter, CB*—thank you for loving me through all of my writer's block, crazy moments, insane deadlines, and sleep-deprived states. I love the two of you more than you could ever possibly understand. Without you, none of this would be possible.

To *my family—my parents, sisters, grandparents, aunts, uncles, and cousins*—thank you for being such a huge part of who I am. Thank you for the lessons you've taught me, the stories you've shared, and the support you've given. Without you, I was just a little girl who may never have believed in herself enough to give this a shot. I love you.

To *Emerald O'Brien, Rachel Renee, and Lauren Lee*—my suspenseful sisters. I'm so incredibly thankful to have you ladies on this journey with me. Thank you for your advice when I'm struggling, your willingness to listen when I need to vent, and your unwavering support in everything I do. I can't wait to see where this beautiful journey takes us and I'm glad we're in it together.

To *my amazing editor, Sarah West*—I've said it before and I'll say it again, you are an absolute super star! The things you manage to catch, your insight, and your dedication to my books and characters is unmatched. I'm forever thankful that we crossed paths.

To *my wonderful proofreaders at My Brother's Editor*—thank you for being my last set of eyes. I'm so grateful for your attention to detail and love of great stories.

To *my Twisted Readers, Street Team, Master List, and Review Team*—you guys are everything to me. I couldn't do this without your support. On a rough day, I can always turn to my groups to make me laugh or encourage me to keep going. Most of you have been here since the beginning and I love you all so much!

To *my beta reader, Emerald (again)*—thank you for being my first words of encouragement when I was sure this book was utter crap. This book is 1000x better thanks to your advice, insight, and questions. Thank you for believing in these characters and pushing me to be better.

And, lastly, to *you*—thank you for purchasing this book and supporting art. Thank you for being a reader. Thank you for every review, every recommendation, every share on social media. Thank you, most of all, for making my dreams come true. Without you, I would just be a girl with a head full of stories and no one to share them with.

ABOUT THE AUTHOR

Kiersten Modglin is an Amazon Top 30 bestselling author of psychological thrillers, a member of International Thriller Writers and the Alliance of Independent Authors, a KDP Select All-Star, and a ThrillerFix Best Psychological Thriller Award Recipient. Kiersten grew up in rural Western Kentucky with dreams of someday publishing a book or two. With more than twenty-five books published to date, Kiersten now lives in Nashville, Tennessee with her husband, daughter, and their two Boston Terriers: Cedric and Georgie. She is best known for her unpredictable psychological suspense. Kiersten's work is currently being translated into multiple languages and readers across the world refer to her as 'The Queen of Twists.' A Netflix addict, Shonda Rhimes super-fan, psychology fanatic, and indoor enthusiast, Kiersten enjoys rainy days spent with her nose in a book.

Sign up for Kiersten's newsletter here:
http://eepurl.com/b3cNFP
Sign up for text alerts from Kiersten here:
www.kierstenmodglinauthor.com/textalerts.html

www.kierstenmodglinauthor.com
www.facebook.com/kierstenmodglinauthor
www.facebook.com/groups/kmodsquad
www.twitter.com/kmodglinauthor
www.instagram.com/kierstenmodglinauthor
www.tiktok.com/@kierstenmodglinauthor
www.goodreads.com/kierstenmodglinauthor
www.bookbub.com/authors/kiersten-modglin
www.amazon.com/author/kierstenmodglin

ALSO BY KIERSTEN MODGLIN

STANDALONE NOVELS

Becoming Mrs. Abbott

The List

The Missing Piece

Playing Jenna

The Beginning After

The Better Choice

The Good Neighbors

The Lucky Ones

The Mother-in-Law

The Dream Job

The Liar's Wife

My Husband's Secret

The Perfect Getaway

The Arrangement

The Roommate

The Missing

Just Married

Our Little Secret

Missing Daughter

THE MESSES SERIES

The Cleaner (The Messes, #1)

The Healer (The Messes, #2)

The Liar (The Messes, #3)

The Prisoner (The Messes, #4)

NOVELLAS

The Long Route: A Lover's Landing Novella

The Stranger in the Woods: A Crimson Falls Novella

THE LOCKE INDUSTRIES SERIES

The Nanny's Secret